BBC
DOCTOR WHO

Diamond Dogs

Also available from BBC Books:

PLAGUE CITY
by Jonathan Morris

THE SHINING MAN
by Cavan Scott

BBC

DOCTOR WHO

Diamond Dogs

Mike Tucker

BBC
BOOKS

3 5 7 9 10 8 6 4

BBC Books, an imprint of Ebury Publishing
20 Vauxhall Bridge Road,
London SW1V 2SA

BBC Books is part of the Penguin Random House group of companies
whose addresses can be found at global.penguinrandomhouse.com

Penguin
Random House
UK

Doctor Who is a BBC Wales production for BBC One.
Executive producers: Steven Moffat and Brian Minchin

First published by BBC Books in 2017

www.eburypublishing.co.uk

Editorial Director: Albert DePetrillo
Copyeditor: Steve Tribe
Series consultant: Justin Richards
Cover design: Lee Binding © Woodlands Books Ltd, 2017
Production: Alex Merrett

A CIP catalogue record for this book is available from the British Library

ISBN 9781785942693

Printed and bound in Great Britain by Clays Ltd, St Ives PLC

Penguin Random House is committed to a sustainable future for our business, our readers
and our planet. This book is made from Forest Stewardship Council® certified paper.

For Sue and Steve

Prologue

The rings of Saturn were a sight that Laura Palmer would never tire of. She had been 23 when she caught her first glimpse of them, a rookie travelling back from her first off-world assignment. She had been one year into her Federation Security training, seconded to a military pacification battalion to gain what her squad commander had charmingly referred to as 'nuts on the ground experience'. That had meant dealing with an Ogron incursion into Federation space; a half-hearted attack on the food supply shuttle delivering grain to the Davy Crockett colony in the Sirius-B system. Dealing with it had been so swift and unsophisticated that her fellow recruits seemed to regard it as little more than boisterous recreation. As far as Laura had been concerned it amounted to a total waste of her time, and had almost resulted in her dropping out of the Security Programme altogether. It was what had happened on her way back to Earth that had changed her mind.

The convoy that she was travelling with had made an unscheduled repair and refuelling stop at Titan. Micrometeorites had punctured the outer casing of the plasma disbursement fins of several ships whilst they were traversing the Kuiper Belt, and there had been a very real danger of catastrophic warp derailment if the damage wasn't dealt with swiftly. When the announcement came from the flight deck that their journey back home was going to be delayed by nearly seven hours, Laura could have screamed with frustration, but when her troopship had dropped out of hyperspace around Saturn, a single glance out of the viewport next to her seat had changed her life for ever.

Laura was familiar with Saturn of course – she had seen enough documentaries and security training films over the years – but nothing had prepared her for the sheer, breathtaking majesty of the planet up close. The gas giant itself had been impressive enough – a vast glowing ball, its surface dimly reflecting the glow of the distant sun, lightning storms crackling and flashing deep in the depths of the monumental cloudscape – but it was the rings that had made the breath catch in her throat.

They soared round the planet like wings – huge, ethereal, impossibly vast. It had only been when the other recruits around her had started to laugh and jeer that she realised that her jaw was literally hanging open with awe.

Seven hours that had initially seemed like a life sentence of boredom went past in a heartbeat. Whilst her crewmates paced the central corridor of the troop carrier, cursing and whining, poking fun and trying to goad her into responding, Laura had sat as if glued to her seat, face pressed to the viewport, watching the kaleidoscopic display of ice crystals and rock tumble and spin with a grace and elegance that she would never have believed possible.

When the repairs were finally complete and the troopship had started to move out of orbit ready to make the warp jump to Earth, the ache of longing that she felt when the rings slid from her view had been almost too much for her to bear. It was at that point she vowed that she would return to Saturn. Return and live there.

Once back on Earth, Laura hurled herself into her training, spectacularly outperforming her fellow recruits over the next three years and ultimately graduating from the Federation Academy with Honours. That gave her the pick of the security assignments that the Federation had to offer, so it had come as something of a surprise to her commanding officer when she requested assignment to Kollo-Zarnista Facility 27.

Laura could still recall the look of bemusement on his face when he had summoned her to his office. Frank Gammadoni had been good to her during her years at the

Academy, and it was only fair that she provided him with the explanation that he obviously wanted.

The Datapad sitting on his desk was active with her request for assignment, unsigned but obviously not unread, when she entered his office. As he gestured for her to sit down, he had picked it up and read through it again.

'Kollo-Zarnista?' A well-manicured eyebrow had risen slowly in bemused disbelief. 'Palmer, are you aware of what that facility is?'

'Yes, sir.'

'Well, I'm going to tell you anyway. It's a dead end. It's a babysitting job, it is so far beneath your ability that I can't even—'

'It's not *what* the facility is, sir.' To this day Laura still couldn't believe that she'd had the nerve to interrupt him like that. 'It's *where* it is.'

'Ah …' A look of understanding had flickered across Colonel Gammadoni's face. 'Saturn.'

'Sir, if you will allow me to explain—'

'There's no need.' This time it was the Colonel's turn to interrupt. Placing the Datapad back on the desk, he had pushed back his chair, and walked to the huge picture window that looked out across the rain lashed skyscrapers of New York City. Several seconds had passed before he spoke, his Italian-American accent warm and mellow.

'I must have been about your age when I got my first glimpse of Saturn. I was a volunteer aboard one of the construction tugs assigned to the reconstruction of the Titan refuelling platform after the great fire of 5012. Have you ever been to Titan, Palmer?'

He hadn't waited for her reply.

'It's brown. All of it. The corridors of the bases, the uniforms, the ground, the sky, the very air … brown. The three months I spent there were the closest thing to living in hell that I ever want to experience.'

He had paused for a second, lost in thirty-year-old memories.

'My gang boss must have just got fed up with looking at my miserable face for day on end. Crocker was quite a character, bald as a coot, one eye missing and with a jerry-rigged pneumatic arm that went wrong practically on a weekly basis. He'd been out on the frontier his entire adult life. One day he just grabbed me by the collar with that rusty old arm of his, bundled me into a shuttle pod, and took me up to see the rings.'

The Colonel had paused again, then without a further word had turned, lifted the Datapad from his desk and stamped it with his digital signature.

'Assignment approved.'

That had been four years ago, and Laura was about to start her fourth tour of duty as the Federation Security Liaison Officer to the Kollo-Zarnista Mining Operation. Her fourth year living and working around Saturn. And unfortunately, her fourth visit to Titan. The problem was that in order to get to Saturn, you had to spend time here first. Laura had come in on one of the deep-space transporters late last night. As soon as she had landed she had presented her ID to the base supervisor, handed her kitbag over to the shuttle loading crews, and registered her g-Taser with the base security mainframe. Then she went down to the rec level to kill the hours until the shuttle picked her up for the last leg of her journey ...

As Laura stepped through the door of the gloomy company bar, several grizzled heads looked up in hopeful expectation, and then looked away almost as quickly as soon as they caught sight of the Federation Security Service badge on her cap and the dark stubby shape of the g-Taser on her belt. Sometimes the fear of authority was a blessing.

She grabbed a menu off the bar and ordered a salt beef sandwich and a beer. The barman barely made eye contact with her, pouring her beer in silence, and handing over the rather limp-looking sandwich with a look of nervous mistrust. He obviously didn't like having security personnel in his bar.

Paying for the meal with the chip in her wrist, Laura took a long gulp of her beer. Thirst slated, she crossed to a window seat, pulled off her cap, and shook her hair loose. She glanced around at her surroundings and smiled. Colonel Gammadoni had been dead right about one thing: Titan was indeed brown. The construction teams had tried their best to disguise the prefabricated modules and bare rock walls of the facility, but a corporate lack of imagination permeated everything, from furniture to colour scheme to signage.

Taking another sip of her beer, her gaze drifted to the vista outside the thick, triple-glazed window, watching the thick fog drift sluggishly across the rust-brown dunes of Titan. She craned her neck, peering up past the spinning radar dishes and untidy aerial arrays that ringed the edge of the base. High above those murky, pendulous clouds was Saturn.

She closed her eyes. Only a few hours to go …

It was only when the harsh blaring noise of the embarkation klaxon jolted her upright that Laura realised she had dropped off to sleep. Cursing her lack of discipline, she scrambled from the table, snatching up her cap and pushing the uneaten sandwich to one side. She hurried across the bar and out into the corridor. A dozen or so mining personnel were making their way towards the shuttle bay, amongst them were a couple of familiar figures. She jogged to catch up with them.

'Jenny! Arcon!'

'Laura.' Jenny Flowers gave her a huge hug. 'I didn't think you'd be back so soon.'

'Are you kidding?' Arcon grinned and tousled her hair with a massive hand. 'This one would never leave if she could get away with it.'

Laura slapped the big African's hand away in mock irritation. 'At least I come back because I want to. Every year you tell me you're going to leave for something better and every year when I get back, here you are.'

'Ah, well this year it's going to be different.' Arcon tapped at a patch on his overalls.

Laura peered at the badge and raised an eyebrow. 'Someone was stupid enough to promote you to Supervisor?'

'A woman of great taste and discretion.' Arcon flashed a grin at Jenny. Jenny was a senior manager at Kollo-Zarnista Mining, and it was a badly kept secret that she and Arcon had been an item for some time.

Laura gave Arcon a hug. 'That's great, I'm pleased for you.' The significance of the promotion suddenly hit her. 'So, you really *are* going to be leaving Saturn?'

Arcon shrugged. 'No supervisor vacancies here. Not unless Delitsky is planning on retiring sometime soon. There are openings on the Jupiter operation.'

'Or Neptune, if the rumours are to be believed,' said Jenny with worried sigh, obviously not thrilled about the prospect.

Arcon's cheery manner evaporated. 'Neptune is never going to happen,' he snapped.

There was an awkward pause. Laura said nothing. The truth was she had seen the security assessments for a potential diamond mine on Neptune and it was a far more likely proposition than Arcon realised. It was also predicted to be the most dangerous assignment in the solar system, and Federation officials were already balking at the potential costs of maintaining a security presence then. If it went ahead, Jenny would have every right to be worried about his safety.

Any further conversation on the topic was halted as a warning siren sounded and, with a hiss of hydraulics, the huge pressure doors in front of them started to slide open, revealing the shuttle beyond. The ship was ancient; its once pristine hull pitted with the scars from dozens of meteorite hits and caked with the dark brown mud that covered the surface of Titan.

The massive doors hit their stops with a thump that shook the floor. The little crowd of impatient passengers bustled forward, making their way through the tangle of umbilical cables that snaked across the hangar and up the steep loading ramp that jutted from the belly of the shuttle.

Promising to catch up with Jenny and Arcon once she had reported in, Laura hurried to her assigned seat and strapped herself in. The pilot was obviously on a tight schedule, because no sooner had the ground crew checked the last person on board than the cabin lights dimmed and the loading ramp started to retract. The second that it locked into place, a harsh electronic voice echoed around the shuttle interior.

'*All ground personnel please vacate immediately. Depressurisation countdown in progress. Repeat. Depressurisation countdown in progress.*'

A few moments later, the shuttle vibrated violently as the last traces of breathable atmosphere in the hangar were vented into space, and Laura felt the familiar lurch in her stomach as the launch pad started its climb towards the airlock doors that separated the hangar from the toxic atmosphere of Titan.

Reaching into her jacket pocket, she removed her comms unit and slipped the tiny bud into her right ear, tuning the frequency to that of flight control. Immediately the chatter between the shuttle pilot and the traffic control team filled her ears, drowning out all other noise. Laura adjusted the volume so that it was a little more background. Monitoring traffic control was by no means part of her duties, but it had become something of a prelaunch ritual for her. A perk of the job, she liked to think.

'*Transport shuttle Glamorgan, this is Titan flight control. All lights green on my board. Launch window is clear. Kollo-Zarnista guidance beacon is activated.*'

'*Thank you, Titan. Umbilicals retracted. Raising radiation flare shields now.*'

'*Roger that, Glamorgan. Retracting main hangar doors in five. Four. Three. Two. One. You are clear for launch. Have a good flight.*'

With a deafening roar that drowned out the voices in Laura's ear, the shuttle's main engines ignited and she was pressed back into the padding of her seat as the little spacecraft launched itself into the thick Titan clouds.

Laura shifted her attention to the tiny porthole alongside her. Clouds of vapour and streams of liquid methane streaked across the window as the shuttlecraft tore itself free of the atmosphere. Gradually the choking clouds started to thin out and then, abruptly, the clouds were gone and there was nothing but blackness and stars beyond the window.

The star-scape started to slide across her field of view as the shuttle banked, and Laura held her breath, waiting for the sight that she had been dreaming of for the last three months.

Slowly the planet came into view. Vast. Beautiful. Like nothing else in the solar system. Saturn and its rings.

Laura let out her breath with a deep, contented sigh.

She was home.

Chapter

1

Kollo-Zarnista Mining Facility 27 hung ugly and motionless amongst the swirling clouds of Saturn. Nearly a quarter of a mile across, it was home to over three hundred miners and support personnel and had now been in almost constant operation for over fifteen years.

In design it was little more than a vast, thick disc, twenty storeys high, the smooth, featureless hull broken only by the four chunky gravity inverters set at equidistant points along its circumference. Pinecone-like in appearance, the strange, bulbous shapes of the huge machines were totally at odds with the construction of the rest of the station, the unfamiliar lines betraying the non-human origins of their design. Each inverter was made up of a series of overlapping plates that constantly tilted and turned as they compensated for the immense gravitational grip of the planet below, their ceaseless movement occasionally revealing a sickly yellow/green light glowing deep within the alien machines.

Tucked in tight beneath the main disc was the mine-head itself, an untidy tangle of command and support modules, dominated by the four vast winches that formed the core of the facility.

Inside the main control room, Rig Chief Jorgen Delitsky glanced impatiently at his watch as the seconds ticked down relentlessly towards the start of mining operations for the day. The shuttle was running behind schedule, and that would result in the mine starting its first shift behind schedule too. Today was not a good day for that to happen.

He glanced across to where Nettleman and Rince were standing at the main control bank. The two Kollo-Zarnista senior executives had arrived the day before yesterday to conduct what they kept referring to as an 'urgent investigation', but as far as Delitsky was concerned they had done nothing but get in the way and waste everyone's time since they got here. They had demanded a tour of the facility, had called dozens of meetings with senior managers to go through figures and review security arrangements, and spent the rest of the time asking for coffee every five minutes and generally distracting his people from their work.

Even now, when everyone should be concentrating on their duties, the two company men were chatting with his extraction team as if they were all at some fancy drinks reception. Claire Robbins, currently on scanning duty, had barely glanced at her screens in the last ten minutes. It was time to put a stop to it.

'Robbins!' Delitsky's voice was like a whip-crack across the room.

Robbins jumped, swinging her chair back to the controls that she had been neglecting with a wince. 'Sorry, Chief.'

Delitsky was pleased to see the smiles drop from the faces of Nettleman and Rince. It was time for them to learn who was really in charge around here. 'I'm still waiting for an ETA on that shuttle docking!'

'On it.'

She busied herself with the controls. 'Shuttle locked on beacon. Gravity funnel holding steady. Docking expected at zero plus seven.'

Delitsky gave a frown of irritation. Seven minutes behind schedule. That wasn't going to look good for any of them. He turned to the small figure in grey overalls perched at the control console next to him. Jenloz was their designated Cancri liaison for the mine, responsible for the maintenance and operation of all the non-human equipment. He was also currently Acting Chief Engineer.

'Anything we can do to speed them up, Jenloz?'

The little Cancri looked at him inquisitively. 'Meaning?'

'You know exactly what I mean,' Delitsky muttered under his breath. 'Tweak the settings on the gravity funnel, bring that shuttle in a little bit faster.'

Jenloz tutted theatrically, amusement making his startling green eyes sparkle like emeralds. 'Really, Chief? You know how strict the rules are with regard to gravity compensation procedures. Are you sure you want to break them with the company bigwigs watching?'

Delitsky gave a wry grin. 'It might be worth it to see their faces when they realise that the shuttle is coming into the docking cradle at maximum speed, but no, you're probably right.'

'A slight adjustment might be possible, Chief. Let me see what I can do to shave a few minutes off the ETA.'

'That's great, Jenloz. Let Tobins know what you're doing.'

Gerry Tobins was the longstanding pilot of the *Glamorgan*, and Delitsky knew that he wouldn't mind bending a few rules if it helped his punctuality figures.

As the little Cancri busied himself making adjustments to the gravity controls, Delitsky turned to face the rest of his crew. 'Listen up, people. We're expecting docking confirmation in the next five to seven minutes. I want all ionisation crews ready to spark up as soon as that confirmation comes in. No excuses!'

The control room was suddenly alive with activity as the crew settled into a familiar routine. Deliberately ignoring the two company executives, Delitsky made his way down the short stairwell to the command pod, slipping into one of the seats and fitting a comms bud into his ear.

In the brightly lit hangar below him, the squat grey shape of the mining bell sat in its support cradle, waiting for the hatch below to open, and the long descent into the Saturnian atmosphere to begin. Like the mine itself, the spherical pod featured the pinecone-like inverters that bulged from the metal skin like some strange, alien fungus, glowing with that unhealthy green inner light. Boiler-suited technicians scurried around the sphere like ants, checking fittings, making adjustments.

Delitsky flicked a switch on the communication console in front of him. 'You all right in there, Baines?'

'Oh, sure. You know how much I love my pressure armour. That's why I named it!'

Delitsky grinned. The two dozen men and women specially trained for the extreme-depth diamond mining all had a peculiar love-hate relationship with the Cancri-designed pressure armour that they had to work in. They referred to themselves as 'the Diamond Dogs', and each of them had customised their individual suits of armour with lurid and crude graffiti – much to the disgust of Jenloz. Roger Baines had painted his suit a vivid red, with the words 'Queen Bitch' emblazoned across the shoulders. Delitsky was convinced that the Cancri's insistence that an elevated pressure level was maintained inside the suits was purely because he was unhappy with this disrespect of his equipment.

Delitsky recalled that Baines had actually argued that the suits were an unnecessary additional precaution given the extreme safety testing that the mining bells themselves went through, but Federation insurance brokers and Kollo-Zarnista health and safety officers all insisted on the double redundancy feature, and having seen first-hand what the pressures of Saturn were capable of, Delitsky wasn't about to argue with them.

Baines's voice crackled in his ear once more. *'What's the holdup, Chief? Shouldn't we have been under way by now?'*

'Shuttle's late. Blame Tobins.'

Baines cursed loudly. *'The sooner Tobins gets that transfer to the outer rim that he keeps banging on about, the better.'*

'I hear you.'

A light on the communications panel started to blink, and Delitsky tapped at the bud in his ear, changing channels. 'I hope you have good news for me, Robbins,' he growled.

'The Glamorgan's *just docked, Chief. Shuttle bay crew are locking it down now.'*

'That's what I wanted to hear.' Delitsky tapped the ear bud again, leaning forward and barking into the microphone in front of him. 'All crew, this is Delitsky.' His voice boomed from speakers around the control room. 'The transport shuttle has already put us behind schedule, so I don't want any of you giving me reasons that will make that situation any worse. All prep teams clear the hangar. Ionisation teams, commence countdown.'

He shut off the microphone and leaned back in his seat, watching the crew in the hangar bay below him hurrying to their stations, closing the huge pressure doors behind them. In the background a harsh electronic countdown had started, and telemetry had begun to stream across the screens on the instrument panels hanging above him. At the console across from him he could see Johanna Teske, the medical officer, peering intently at the bio-readouts being relayed from the mining pod, monitoring Baines's vital signs for any anomalies.

Delitsky liked Teske. She was the only one on the station remotely close to his age, and one of the few who shared his desire to see that everything was done properly. Not like those two clowns from head office. They were only interested in getting things done cheaply.

He craned his neck to see where the two managers had got to. Thankfully they had seated themselves in the observation gallery, well out of the way of his crew who were now fully engaged with their duties. Delitsky nodded with satisfaction. Good. With luck that meant they would stay out of his way for the next few hours.

Turning his attention back to the task in hand, he cast a practised eye over the instruments. From the look of things, the slight delay would only have a minimal impact on their schedule. Jenloz had obviously done a good job speeding up the shuttle arrival. He made a mental note to ensure that the little Cancri got a little extra in his bonus.

He swiped a hand over the meteorological diagnostic controls. The storm below the mine was really moving. He tapped his ear bud again. 'I hope you strapped in tight, Baines. Looks like it's going to be a little lively down there.'

'You know me, Chief. Always up for a challenge.'

'Glad to hear it.'

Delitsky closed his eyes, listening to the mechanical voice of the station mainframe as it counted down inexorably towards zero. This was where things got real. And dangerous. All levity faded from the Rig Chief's voice. 'All right, Baines. Stand by. We're initiating drop in … Five. Four. Three. Two. One. Drop.'

Through the armoured glass, Delitsky watched as the hangar doors snapped open and the grey sphere vanished into the boiling clouds of Saturn.

At the same moment, the entire station shuddered as the ionisation satellites seeded through the planet's atmosphere flared into life, sending lightning arcing through the clouds.

A short time later it started to rain diamonds.

Chapter

2

The upper level of Kollo-Zarnista Mining Facility 27 housed the vault – a vast chamber filled with the diamonds extracted from the crushing atmosphere of the planet below. Here in this huge room there was more wealth than on the rest of the planets in the solar system combined.

Not that you would guess from its appearance. The floors, the walls, the ceiling of the vault were all a flat, uniform grey. The tube-train-sized cylindrical containers that radiated around the walls seemed unremarkable. Unremarkable save for the huge quantities of Saturnian diamonds that each of them held.

These stones were the lifeblood on which the ever-expanding empire of the human race depended. Without them the species may not have even survived, trapped for ever in a backwater of the galaxy with ever-diminishing resources. There were no precious metals left on Earth, Homo sapiens had stripped their home planet bare almost before they had taken their first steps into the universe. Mars and Venus had soon followed and, with Mercury offering no discernible benefits to mankind, the masters of Earth had turned their attention to the gas giants instead.

The possibility that the atmosphere of Saturn and Jupiter harboured an untapped source of precious stones had been theorised as far back as the early twenty-first century, but reaching them was an entirely different matter. The initial attempts to extract the wealth from these behemoths of the solar system had not gone well. Mission after mission ended in disaster: hundreds of lives were lost, men, women and equipment vanishing for ever into the swirling clouds, dragged down by the monstrous gravitational forces of the huge planets, and crushed out of existence.

But, like the gold prospectors of antiquity, the miners were undaunted, spurred on by the promise of untold wealth if they were successful, and the increasing desperation of a planetary elite that sensed their imminent extinction if these new resources could not be exploited.

Salvation came in the form of the Cancri, an alien race from beyond Cygnus-A, who arrived (unlike so many alien races that stumbled across the Earth) with no threats of destruction or dreams of conquest, but purely with an offer of assistance.

For a price, of course.

The Cancri were also expanding into the universe, and they too had started to exhaust their home worlds. What they did have, however, was a mastery of pressure and gravity. To the scientists of Earth, the technology they brought was advanced to the point that they could barely understand it. But it was exactly what they needed if they were going to make any headway in extracting the diamond wealth that the human race so desperately needed.

And so, a partnership was agreed, a business deal between the two planets, and Saturn was agreed on to be the first test site. The Cancri would provide the knowledge of how to create new alloys that could survive the crushing pressures of the gas giant and the gravitic machinery needed to keep a mine safely in orbit within that atmosphere. They would also give the technical support needed to keep that machinery functioning, whilst Earth would provide the labour force. As payment for their services, the Cancri would take a percentage of the diamonds mined, although only a few people high up in the corridors of power knew exactly what proportion of the wealth the Cancri leaders had managed to negotiate.

The truth was – as many experts had pointed out over the years, when the question of how much the Cancri were taking became a political sore point – whatever proportion it was, it was worth it. Without the Cancri gravity inverters, there would be no diamonds; without the diamonds, the expansion of the Human Empire would grind to a halt.

And so the partnership had blossomed. As well as the mines on Saturn there were now diamond extraction facilities on Jupiter and, if the colonies on the rim worlds continued to grow at the current rate, there would soon be the need to start operations on Neptune as well.

The success of the Human-Cancri partnership did not come without its problems, however. The transportation of such vast wealth from the mines to the home worlds inevitably attracted the attention of those who found it easier to acquire the diamonds *without* going to the trouble of mining for them. Time and time again, diamond shipments were raided, either on the way to Earth or to Cancri, until finally the losses to jewel thieves became so great that the governments of both planets agreed that a solution had to be found.

Once again, it was the Cancri gravity inverters that provided a solution to the problem. Initially diamond shipments had been on a weekly schedule, on the assumption that the sooner they were removed from the mine environment, the safer they would be. It was a young Federation security officer called Gammadoni who had pointed out that it was the cargo transporters that were the weak point. Given their locations, the mines *themselves* were actually the safest places to store the diamonds. Without a gravity inverter, there was no way of reaching them, and given that only the Cancri had the ability to make such machines …

The new policy was swiftly adopted, and the mines were re-engineered to also act as vaults, storing the diamonds in huge strong rooms, safe from pirates and marauders.

The vault on Kollo-Zarnista Facility 27 was almost full. Soon the high-security exercise of shipping the diamonds would begin, but for the moment the chamber was quiet and empty, the only noise in the cavernous chamber a slight vibration caused by the Cancri gravity inverters: a vibration that caused the diamonds to give off a faint, almost musical tinkle as they shifted inside their cold, metal containers.

That musical tinkling was slowly drowned out by a new sound – a harsh, elephantine trumpeting – and a new container joined the others in the vault, slowly materialising in the exact centre of the massive circular chamber. The new addition was small, blue and rectangular and had the words 'POLICE PUBLIC CALL BOX' emblazoned on a sign above its doors. An Earth historian might have recognised it as a primitive communication artefact from the planet's pre-space-age era, but they would have been wrong. Behind those rickety-looking wooden doors was one of the most sophisticated time-space machines ever constructed – a TARDIS, a time ship from the planet Gallifrey, capable of travelling to any world in any point in history. This particular TARDIS was the property of a

Time Lord known simply as the Doctor and, a few seconds after it had appeared, one of the doors was snatched open and the face of the Doctor peered out into the gloom.

In this incarnation (the first of his brand new life cycle), the Doctor was tall, thin and gangly-limbed, with unruly grey hair and vast, endlessly expressive eyebrows. Satisfied that he had landed in the correct location, he stepped out of the TARDIS and calling back over his shoulder.

'Come on, out you come. The quicker we get this over with, the quicker we can get back.'

Another figure appeared in the doorway. Bill was tall and slim, with a shock of jet-black curly hair and a bright, inquisitive expression. She looked around the darkened room warily. She had started to get used to the fact that travelling in the TARDIS with the Doctor inevitably meant landing in the middle of something dangerous. Only recently she had been stalked by emoticon robots on a distant planet in the far future and nearly eaten by an alien fish in Victorian London.

She stepped nervously from the TARDIS. 'Where are we?'

'Saturn.' The Doctor didn't look up.

'Saturn. Right.' Bill rolled her eyes. 'Nardole is going to give you a right ticking off when he finds out.'

'Well, he's not going to find out if you don't tell him.'

Bill gave a snort. 'He's going to realise eventually. You can't keep sneaking off without him noticing.'

The Doctor extended a bony finger towards the TARDIS. 'Time machine, remember? We can be back before he knows we've gone.'

'Yeah, and he knows that too. He's not stupid.'

'No, but he is easily distracted, and I've left him a copy of this month's *Good Food* magazine with a pull-out section on things you can make with Rice Krispies.'

Bill shrugged, admitting defeat. 'Yeah, that'll do the trick.' Shivering in the cold air, she zipped up her denim jacket, thrusting her hands into the pockets and looking around the room. 'Not impressed by Saturn,' she sniffed.

'Ah, but you should be.' The Doctor turned, spinning on his heel, throwing his arms wide. 'If you only knew what most people would give to be standing where you are standing right now.'

Bill looked around in bemusement. 'In a big empty room?'

'Ah, but the room isn't empty, is it?'

Bill shrugged. 'OK, a room full of big cylinders. Still not getting my pulse racing.'

'Well then, maybe you should be asking yourself what's *inside* the cylinders.'

With that the Doctor made a beeline for one of the huge containers, squatted down in front of it and slipped on his sonic sunglasses. Bill sighed. He was obviously not going to give her a straight answer as to why they were here, so she might as well just sit tight and let him get on with it.

The sooner they got whatever they were after, the sooner they could get out of here.

Several floors below them, in the Main Security Control room, Laura Palmer was slowly making her way through the dozens of reports and memos that had built up since her last tour of duty. As usual, most of them were fairly routine, but Laura was concerned to note that there had been an increase in the number of reports of unscheduled craft in the area.

She sipped at her coffee, a frown creasing her brow. That was cause for concern. Piracy was a very real worry amongst her superiors. Initially they had had a problem with the diamonds being targeted when they were in transit to Earth, usually just as the cargo shuttles were coming out of warp, but the increasing volume of security ships in that sector had forced the pirates to start looking for other options. Two years ago, the transport shuttle from Titan had been shadowed by a Zzinbriizi stealth ship that had tried to follow it to the Kollo-Zarnista facility itself. They might have made it too, if the pilot hadn't been careless and slipped out of the gravity funnel. That had resulted in them taking a very fast one-way trip into the centre of Saturn.

Not that it had stopped others from trying, or course. The potential rewards from making a successful raid on a diamond transport ship were so huge that even seemingly suicidal risks were deemed worth taking. The gangs now working around the gas giants were amongst the best-funded in the solar system. And they were starting to attract the attention of criminals from further afield. Laura wasn't sure how her meagre security detail would cope with a concerted attack from someone allied to the likes of Rhom-Dutt or Sharaz Jek ...

'Captain Palmer?'

Laura looked up to see Sergeant Lynne Harrison hovering nervously in front of her, a Datapad grasped tightly in her hands.

'Lynne. Hi. Sorry, I was miles away.' She gestured at the empty chair on the other side of the desk.

Lynne Harrison sat down. She looked worried.

Laura raised an eyebrow. 'Problem, Sergeant?'

'Do you remember during your last tour we discussed the possibility of getting Jenloz to hook up a gravity analyser to the security sensor grid?'

Laura nodded. It had been just after the Zzinbriizi ship had made its failed attempt to board them that they had both come up with the idea. The Cancri required a precise mass reading for the station in order to operate the gravity inverters correctly, and had equipment mounted all over the hull of the mine. It had been Lynne who had pointed out that the same equipment could alert them if someone made an unauthorised landing.

'Don't tell me something followed the shuttle in again?' asked Laura in alarm.

Lynne quickly shook her head. 'No, I don't think so.' She slid the Datapad across the desk. 'I was just making a routine check of the sensor net and the mass readings changed.'

'Changed?'

Laura nodded. 'It's not by much, but it changed as I was watching, otherwise I might not even have noticed it.'

Laura picked up the pad and scrutinised the figures on the screen. The mass increase was infinitesimal, but it was there. 'You're right. About three minutes ago.' Her frown deepened. 'It's not heavy enough to be a ship …'

'Do you want me to sound the general alarm?'

'No.' Laura wasn't going to upset Delitsky this soon after setting foot back on the station, especially given that he was already in a bad mood thanks to the late arrival of the shuttle. If she interrupted the mining with something that could easily be a sensor fault …

She handed the Datapad back to her sergeant. 'Get the mainframe to keep an eye on it. Notify me immediately if the readings change again. As soon as Jenloz gets off shift, have him run a full diagnostic.'

'Yes, sir.' Harrison rose from her seat.

'And, Sergeant …'

'Sir?'

'Check that the Flying Squad are ready to go.'

Harrison looked at her superior officer with mild surprise.

Laura shrugged, aware that she might be overreacting. 'Just in case.'

With a nod, Lynne hurried back towards her station. Laura watched her go. *Was* she overreacting? A nagging suspicion was starting to build in her mind, a suspicion that her return to Saturn wasn't going to be the quiet homecoming that she wanted.

Bill was starting to get seriously bored now. What was the point of hanging around with a man who had a machine capable of travelling anywhere in time and space if they were just going to end up in some dark cold space warehouse? She hadn't even found any windows that she could look out of.

'Saturn …' she snorted contemptuously, stamping her feet to try to ward off the cold.

If the Doctor was aware of her discomfort, then he didn't show it. He was still sitting cross-legged in front of the cylinder. He'd put away his sonic sunglasses and was now prodding at the door with his sonic screwdriver instead. The high-pitched warbling that echoed around the room was setting Bill's teeth on edge.

Patience at an end, Bill stamped over to the Doctor and prodded him in the back with the toe of her boot. 'Are you going to be much longer?'

'Careful!' The Doctor peered up at her reproachfully. 'You could set it off.'

'Set what off?'

'The alarm,' said the Doctor. 'And that would be bad!'

'What alarm?' cried Bill in exasperation. 'If you would just let me know what you're are trying to do!'

'It'll be lot easier if I just show you.'

The Doctor scrambled to his feet. Grasping her by the shoulders, he steered her firmly to one side, then turned to the cylinder and raised the sonic screwdriver once more.

The harsh cricket-like warble filled the air again and, slowly, the front of the cylinder started to swing upwards. As it did so, strip lights inside flickered into life, their harsh white glare making Bill squint after so long in the gloom.

The door clunked to a halt and the Doctor reached inside the cylinder, plucking something small and shiny from one of the racks that lined the curved walls. He shut off his sonic screwdriver and held out the object for Bill to see.

She rubbed at her eyes in disbelief.

It was a diamond.

The cylinder was brimming with diamonds!

Chapter

3

Jorgen Delitsky was a happy man. Despite the late start, the shift was going well. They were already back on schedule, and conditions looked extremely promising for a well above average yield. Out of the corner of his eye he could see the broad smiles on the faces of the two Kollo-Zarnista executives as they studied the readouts that scrolled across the screens in the observation gallery.

That was good news. The sooner they realised that everything was running as it should, the sooner they would leave him in peace. He was about to turn back to his instruments when he caught sight of Johanna Teske making her way across the control room towards him.

Delitsky frowned. It was extremely unusual for Teske to leave her station during a shift.

The medical officer descended the ladder into the control pod with graceful ease and slipped into the chair alongside him. 'You got a moment, Chief?'

That was enough to get Delitsky worried. She *never* called him Chief. He shot a nervous glance back at the observation gallery, but Nettleman and Rince were too busy concentrating on the money that they were making to notice anything else that was going on.

'OK, Doc, what's the story?'

Teske reached for the control desk, her long, elegant fingers tapping at the keyboard as she transferred the medical readout from her own station to one of Delitsky's screens.

'Baines's reading have been getting increasingly erratic over the last ten minutes.'

Delitsky peered at the readout. He was experienced enough to see that Baines's heart rate and pulse were slightly elevated, but there was nothing there that he would deem life-threatening.

He turned to tell Teske as much but before he could open his mouth she cut in. 'Before you tell me that it's nothing, look at this.' Her fingers danced over the controls again, and a graph flashed up onto the screen. She pointed at several jagged peaks on an otherwise smoothly undulating line. 'Three times in the last few minutes there's been sudden spike in heart rate and adrenalin.'

'So, it's been a busy shift. He knows that we were behind schedule and—'

'It's more than that, Jorgen.' Teske interrupted again. 'These readings are unusual. It's as if something is periodically making him jump out of his skin.'

Delitsky had known Johanna Teske a long time. If she thought that there was something wrong, she was worth listening to. Her timing though …

He cursed under his breath. 'Of all the shifts you could have picked …' He tapped his ear bud. 'How you doin' down there, Baines?'

'*Um, I'm good, Chief.*'

Delitsky shot Teske a look. Even over the communicator Baines's voice sounded strained.

'Are you sure? I know how much you hate that armour …'

'*I … It's not the armour.*'

Delitsky swiped at a control, ensuring that the remainder of the conversation couldn't be overheard by anybody else.

'Baines, I'm going to pass you over to the Doc …'

The fact that Baines didn't complain about that was proof enough in Delitsky's mind that something was definitely wrong.

Teske tapped at her own ear bud. 'Baines, it's Dr Teske.'

'*Hi, Doc.*'

'Not too happy with the vitals I'm getting on my screens, big man … Anything going on down there that we should know about?'

There was a pause …

'*Not sure you're going to believe it.*'

Another pause.

'*Not sure I believe it myself.*'

'Try me.'

'I think … I think I'm hearing something outside the bell.'

Bill turned in a slow circle, looking incredulously at the rows of cylinders radiating around her. In her head she was trying to calculate just how many gemstones the room might hold, and her brain was struggling with the numbers. The quantity of uncut diamonds in the chamber was absolutely staggering.

The Doctor, on the other hand, seemed completely at ease. He had pulled an ancient eyeglass from one of the many pockets in his jacket and was intently studying the diamond that he had plucked from the rack.

A sudden realisation struck Bill. The Doctor had been here before.

'Do this a lot, do you?' She cocked her head on one side, one eyebrow raised.

'Hm?' said the Doctor absentmindedly.

'I said, do this a lot, do you?' repeated Bill. 'This breaking and entering lark?'

The Doctor let the eyeglass drop into his hand and turned to face her, the diamond held between thumb and forefinger. 'The trick is to get one exactly the right size. If they're too large, they tend to arouse suspicion.'

'Oh, wow, really?' Bill couldn't keep the sarcasm from her voice. 'You do surprise me. What on earth do you *need* it for?'

'Housekeeping'.

Bill stared at him incredulously. 'Housekeeping?'

'Housekeeping! Nardole seems to go through money at an exorbitant rate. He's always buying things with it. Tea. Milk. Popcorn. Rhubarb. Toilet paper. The list is endless.'

'But that diamond must be worth thousands of pounds!'

'He goes through a lot of toilet paper!'

'But it's *stealing*!'

The Doctor rolled his eyes in exasperation. 'Hardly! I'm just materialising without being detected, picking the lock of one of the vaults in the most secure facility in the solar system and taking one single diamond from a stash of billions. Where's the harm in that?'

Bill folded her arms and glared at him accusingly.

'Look, let me explain,' the Doctor sighed, his voice taking on the authoritative tone that he always used in his lectures. 'The diamonds in this room are nothing more than a by-product of Saturn's atmosphere. In the upper atmosphere, in the thunderstorm alleys, intense lightning turns methane into soot. As the soot falls, the pressure on it increases and it turns into graphite. Get deep enough and the graphite toughens into diamonds.'

Bill couldn't quite believe it. 'So you're saying it literally rains diamonds?'

'Yup.' The Doctor nodded. 'This facility is just like a giant net, scooping them out of the atmosphere.'

'That easy, huh?'

'Yes. Well…not exactly easy. Incredibly difficult and dangerous, in fact. But the income from these diamonds is what drives the entire expansion of the human race into space.'

'And you're quite happy to break in here and nick some of them.'

'Not some!' The Doctor was indignant. 'One.'

'On this occasion.'

'All right! One every now and then.' A sheepish look flickered momentarily across his thin face. 'I suppose I *could* materialise the TARDIS in the lower atmosphere and grab one myself…' The look vanished as quickly as it had arrived. 'But I'm a busy man! Besides, look…' He gestured at the dozens of cylinders ranged around the room. 'Do you seriously think they're going to miss one?'

Bill opened her mouth to argue with him, but immediately thought better of it. Nothing she could say would do anything to change his opinion, so she might as well just save her breath. As far as he was concerned taking the diamond was no different from if she had gone scrumping for apples.

'Fine, whatever.'

Satisfied that he had won the argument, the Doctor slipped the jeweller's glass back into his eye and resumed his examination of the diamond.

Shaking her head, Bill wandered back across the vault until she was standing back in front of the cylinder that the Doctor had opened. She had begun to realise that the Doctor had his own peculiar moral code. A very *alien* moral code, in fact. When it was something big, like saving a planet or defeating some monstrous enemy, then his rules were very clearly defined, but present him with something that he considered small or insignificant …

She took a deep breath, wondering exactly where she sat on that scale of importance. Was she, in fact, just like one of these diamonds, plucked at random from billions?

Billions.

She was still struggling to get her head around the numbers. Diamonds dropping from the sky like rain whilst she was struggling to get by on the wages of a canteen assistant. Just a few of these diamonds would be enough to set her up for life. She'd be able to move out of that room at Moira's, get a place of her own, get a car, get a better job, find a nice girl …

The light was glinting off the surface of the diamonds, and it was making her head swim. Just *one* diamond would change everything. Perhaps the Doctor was right. Perhaps it didn't really matter. No one would ever notice. Just one out of billions.

Before she could properly think about what she was doing, Bill found herself stepping forward, reaching out for one of the glittering stones.

'Bill! No!'

The Doctor's strangled cry echoed like a thunderclap around the chamber, but it was too late. As she shook herself from her daydream, her foot crossed the threshold of the cylinder.

And the world exploded into a cacophony of screeching alarms.

Laura froze in disbelief as the intruder alarm went off. A fraction of a second later, four years of Federation training took over and she launched herself from her chair, snatching the g-Taser from her belt.

'I want two men covering the south lift. Move!' she barked, sending officers scrambling across the room. 'Sergeant Harrison, I want priority override on the main entry locks. Nothing gets in or out of here. You hear me? Nothing.'

'Yes, sir!'

'You two.' She pointed at her two remaining officers. 'With me.'

As Laura raced towards the lift, she reached out and punched a control on a console in the centre of the room. There was a hiss of compressed gas, and four gleaming metal shapes launched themselves upwards through chutes in the ceiling.

The Flying Squad had been dispatched.

The Doctor was staring at Bill. His expression was a mixture of horror and disappointment, and it was that disappointment that she found the hardest to bear.

'I'm sorry,' she cried, stepping away from the cylinder, hands held out in apology. 'I wasn't thinking.'

'Looked to me as though you were thinking a little bit too much.' The Doctor bounded across the room, his sonic screwdriver already in his hand and pointing at the open cylinder. He grabbed Bill by the hand and hauled her out of the way of the door as it slammed shut with a deafening clang. 'I think we should get out of here,' he said, stuffing the screwdriver into his pocket.

Bill nodded. If there were to be any recriminations then the Doctor was obviously going to save them until later.

Still holding on to her hand, the Doctor dragged her towards the TARDIS. They had barely made it six metres when four metal shapes burst through concealed hatches in the floor. The Doctor skidded to a halt.

'Oh …'

Bill stared at the objects. They were spherical, about the size of a football, half a dozen jet-black camera eyes dotted across their polished metal skins. Each of them was emblazoned with a badge and a number, and even though Bill didn't recognise the design, the general appearance left no doubt as to the spheres' function. Bill swallowed hard. 'Police?'

'Security Orbs.' The Doctor, still holding Bill's hand, was backing away from the TARDIS, eyes darting from sphere to sphere as they slowly started to surround them.

'Dangerous?'

'Only if you've broken the law.'

'So only if you've done something incredibly stupid like – oh, I don't know – tried to steal one of the diamonds in this vault?'

'Yes, something like that could make them very unfriendly.'

Out of the corner of her eye, Bill could see that the Doctor was trying to extract his sonic screwdriver from his pocket again, using her body to try and hide what his was doing from the advancing spheres.

'Now listen to me very carefully.' The Doctor released her hand, his voice low and urgent. 'When I tell you to run, you—'

He never finished the sentence.

With lightning speed, one of the spheres darted forward, a thin metal probe whipping from its casing. There was a sharp crack, a blaze of electric blue light, and the Doctor gave a cry of pain, the sonic screwdriver dropping from his numbed fingers and clattering to the floor.

Moments later, there was the noise of booted feet on the metal floor and half a dozen uniformed officers stormed into the vault, each of them holding a snub-nosed blaster pointing unwaveringly at the Doctor and Bill. Wincing at the pain from his singed fingers, the Doctor slowly raised his hands. Bill did the same.

A young woman, the captain's insignia on her uniform marking her out as the officer in change, approached them, her face a mask of incredulous amazement as her gaze went from the Doctor, to Bill, to the TARDIS and then back again.

'Who the hell are you?'

Teske and Delitsky locked eyes.

'Something *outside* the bell ...'

'I know, it sounds crazy, but—'

There was a sudden noise over the comms, loud enough to make Delitsky wince. The graph on the screen spiked alarmingly and Baines's voice went up an octave.

'*Did you hear that? Tell me you heard that too!*'

'We heard some interference, Baines, but that's hardly—'

'*Holy ... It's back! I'm not kidding. There's something outside the bell! I can hear it on the hull!*'

'Baines!' Teske leaned forward over her screens, her voice urgent. 'Roger, I need you to calm down.'

'*Calm down?*' Baines was almost hysterical. '*Did you not hear what I said? THERE IS SOMETHING OUTSIDE THE BELL!*'

Baines's voice was now so loud in Delitsky's ear bud that other people in the control room could hear it. The miner was clearly terrified. Warning lights were already starting to flash urgently on the medical readouts as his heart rate skyrocketed. Several of the crew were already looking up from their controls, casting curious glances towards the control pod. It wasn't going to be long before they started to realise that something was wrong.

'You've gotta do something to calm this craziness down, Johanna,' whispered Delitsky. 'He's going to have a damn heart attack.'

'Roger. Listen to me.' Teske tried to keep her voice calm. 'We both know that what you are saying is impossible. Think about where you are. There cannot be anything outside the bell.'

'*And I'm telling you there is!*'

There was another strange noise, louder than the last.

'*Oh, God! They're trying to open the hatch.*' Baines was screaming now. '*You've got to do something. You've got to—*'

Delitsky and Teske tore the buds from their ears as the comms channel was swamped by a deafening screech of static. Seconds later, alarms started to blare around the control room, and the harsh voice of the mainframe boomed from the speakers.

'*Warning. Mining bell hull integrity compromised. Warning! Mining bell hull integrity compromised.*'

'Get him up!' yelled Delitsky. 'Get him up now!'

Technicians scrambled to operate emergency controls that they had never dreamed would need to be used. Delitsky watched as the four huge winches in the hangar bay below him started to draw the bell inexorably back towards the mine.

'Come on,' he hissed through gritted teeth. 'Come on …'

The entire rig suddenly lurched, sending Delitsky crashing into the control panel. The lights in the control room flickered and a new series of alarms joined their voices to the cacophony.

Delitsky staggered to his feet, clutching at his badly bruised arm. All around him his crew were struggling to get back to their feet. Behind him he could hear the high-pitched voice of Jenloz as he yelled instructions to his team, desperately trying to stabilise the rig.

Delitsky could only stare in disbelief at the winches in the hangar bay. The huge cables were unspooling at impossible speed, sending sparks showering into the air.

It was as if something had a hold of the bell.

Chapter

4

The Doctor had tried his very best to be nice, thought Bill, he really, *really* had. It was just that he wasn't very good at it.

Things had started badly when the security guards had pushed them against a wall and frisked them. And it had got worse as soon as they found the diamond in the Doctor's pocket, which hadn't helped his attempts to convince them that they were just visiting and really didn't mean any harm.

It was when they had started interrogating him about what the TARDIS was and how he had got it in here that things had really started to go downhill. It had reminded Bill of the time during one of the Doctor's lectures that some foolish student had decided to argue with him about his conclusions with regard to cyclical time.

Bill shook her head. Poor Derek. He still couldn't walk past the lecture hall without twitching...

Now the Doctor was pinned up against the wall by two of the security guards, both of whom seemed itching to just shake the information out of him, whilst the spherical robots hovered around his head like angry bees. Bill almost felt sorry for the pretty young commanding officer trying to keep some semblance of order. She really didn't know what she was letting herself in for.

'For the last time, will you just tell us who you are and where your accomplices are.'

'And I keep telling you I don't have any accomplices. I don't need them. I'm clever enough on my own.'

'Really.' Captain Palmer jerked a thumb over her shoulder at the incongruous shape of the TARDIS. 'Well, if you don't have any accomplices then how did you get that in here?'

'And if you would just pay attention to what I am trying to tell you about the interstitial nature of space-time then perhaps it would help you understand that better! But no, you don't want to listen. Typical pudding brains!'

The security guards holding him tightened their grip. Bill could have sworn that one of them actually growled. If the Doctor wasn't careful, he was going to get beaten up. She needed to do something.

She took a step forward, but the woman guarding her, a sergeant called Harrison, placed a firm hand on her shoulder. 'Just stay where you are, miss. Captain Palmer will get to you in due course.'

'But he's going to get hurt.'

'Not if he's sensible.'

Before Bill could tell her that being sensible was the last thing that the Doctor ever did, the entire room suddenly shook alarmingly. The security officers looked at each other in bemusement.

'What the hell was that?'

Without further warning the room lurched, sending everyone reeling. Seizing her chance, Bill tore herself away from Harrison, scrabbling across the tilting floor towards the Doctor.

'Stop her!'

Half a dozen pairs of hands reached out to grab her, but the floor suddenly heaved again and Bill felt herself falling, sliding. She scrabbled for a handhold, but the metal floor was like an ice rink. Realising that there was nothing she could do to stop herself, she clasped her hands over her head and tucked into a ball.

She crashed against the wall with an impact that almost shook the teeth from her head. Around her, the shuddering and vibrating was slowly starting to subside, and Bill realised that if she was going to make the most of the confusion then the moment was now. Clutching at her bruised elbow she scrambled to her feet.

'Doctor?'

'Right behind you.'

Grateful to hear his voice, Bill turned. The Doctor was already on his feet, and had one of the snub-nosed blasters in his hand.

It was pointed directly at her head.

'Delitsky!'

Nettleman's voice snapped Delitsky from his daze. The company official was staring down into the control pit. He had a nasty-looking bruise on his forehead.

'What the hell is happening?'

'I wish I knew.'

Delitsky clambered up the ladder and pushed past him, hurrying over to where Jenloz was barking orders to the gravity control team.

'Jenloz! Are we stabilised?'

The little Cancri turned and unleashed a stream of clicks and squeals that even Delitsky could tell was not well meant.

'Don't get snarky with me,' snapped the Rig Chief. 'Just give me some answers.'

'Gravity inverters are recalibrated and holding.' Jenloz glared at him. 'But if we get another shaking like that ...'

'Right.' Delitsky turned to his crew. 'We have an emergency situation here, and I want everyone except essential staff to clear the room.'

A dozen or more people immediately got up and started to file calmly from the room.

'I hope that doesn't include Mister Nettleman and myself,' said Rince, hurrying forwards and squinting at him through his glasses.

'No, Mister Rince,' Delitsky interrupted him. 'I'm certain that your "expertise" will be of great assistance.'

Pushing Rince out of the way, Delitsky crossed to Jo Teske. The medic was still trying to get through to Baines in the bell.

'Baines, do you read me? Baines!'

'What's going on down there, Jo?'

'I don't know.' Teske was obviously at a loss; Delitsky had never seen her like this before. 'Just look at the life signs.'

She pointed at the screen. Baines's vital signs had peaked alarmingly at the moment they had lost contact with him, and then dropped to levels that even Delitsky could tell were a long, *long* way from normal.

'Is he still alive?'

'I have no idea, Jorgen. I've never seen life signs like this in my life before. All I do know is that we need to get him back up here, and we need to do it quickly.'

That was all Delitsky needed. He turned to his expectant crew.

'OK, we're going to perform an emergency retract.'

That raised a few eyebrows, but Delitsky quickly silenced the murmurs that started to echo around the room.

'I'm aware that none of you will ever have done this outside of a simulator before. Well, guess what? Neither have I. But there is a procedure; we just have to follow it. Now please get to your stations and get ready.'

As Delitsky made his way back to his command position, Nettleman intercepted him, blocking his way. Delitsky stopped, not bothering to hide the distaste in his eyes.

'Mister Nettleman, if you don't mind?'

'Did I hear you right? You're going to initiate an emergency retract?'

'You heard right.'

'Can I remind you, Chief Delitsky, that an emergency retract procedure will require you to jettison all mining outriggers from the bell.'

'I am well aware of that.'

'But you can't …'

'I can see no other option.'

Nettleman leaned uncomfortably close to him; Delitsky could smell the sweat on the man's skin. 'But that will mean the loss of the diamonds,' he hissed. 'You must find an alternative.'

Delitsky stared back at him with nothing but contempt. 'I don't give a damn about the diamonds! I've got a man in trouble down there, and in my opinion an emergency retract gives us the best option of recovering him alive.'

'Do I have to order you?'

'Mister Nettleman, in an emergency situation all decisions relating to the safety of the mine and its crew devolve to the Rig Chief. *All* decisions. Now, either you get out of my way and let me do my job, or I will use that authority to call security and have you removed from this control room.'

Nettleman's expression went from shock, to anger then embarrassment as he realised that he had no other option than to step out of the way.

'Thank you,' said Delitsky curtly, making his down the short ladder into the control position. He took his seat, aware that he had just made a very powerful enemy. 'Anybody not ready to do this?'

There were no dissenting voices.

'All right.' He took a deep breath. 'Pod control. Jettison all outriggers.'

A seldom-lit row of indicator lights went red on the panel in front of him. Not much fanfare when you realised that they indicated that three million dollars' worth of diamonds had just been dumped into the atmosphere below.

'Retract comms antennae.'

Another row of lights.

'Flatten profile of pod gravity inverters.'

The final row of lights went red.

'Close shutters.'

A series of huge steel shutters slid into place over the observation windows, cutting off the view of the hangar. To Delitsky, they only served to reinforce just how dangerous the operation they were about to attempt was. Personally, he'd rather see the danger than imagine it.

'Retract.'

Delitsky braced himself. If whatever was below them still had the pod in its grip, he would have to take more extreme action. But this time there was only a slowly escalating whine as the four winches in the hangar below came up to maximum speed.

He could hear Robbins reading off the countdown as the pod was dragged back towards them. 'Seven hundred metres. Six hundred. Four hundred. Three hundred.' She was having to shout above the terrifying noise from the winches now.

'Jenloz. Talk to me!' bellowed Delitsky.

'Holding stable.' The little engineer's voice was barely audible over the noise.

'Two hundred. One Hundred. Zero.'

The rig lurched as the emergency brakes were applied and the pod slammed into the hangar.

'Engage airlock.'

Delitsky was already out of his seat before the confirmation came. 'Open those damn shutters and get an emergency crew in there!'

With a whirr of motors, the shutters started to retract, revealing the pod sitting somewhat drunkenly in the hangar. Stripped of all its external probes and fixtures it looked even more like an egg than before.

As Delitsky watched, the airlock doors slid open and an emergency crew, clad in protective suits, rushed forward, cutting gear ready in case it was needed.

Delitsky urged them on. 'Hurry it up, hurry it up.'

The team leader hauled himself up onto the side of the pod, reaching out with heavy gloves to pull the emergency release handle that would release the hatch. With agonising slowness the heavy, armoured hatch swung open.

The team leader leaned forward, peering into the interior of the pod. Then he stopped, seemingly frozen.

'What is it?' yelled Delitsky. 'Is he OK?'

The rescue worker looked up wordlessly from the hangar, his face pale with shock. He stepped back from the hatch allowing Delitsky a clear view into the interior.

It was empty.

Chapter

5

Laura had dealt with plenty of hostage situations in her career, but the one confronting her was not like any that she had had to deal with before.

As soon as the station had stopped shaking, the tall man – the Doctor, he had called himself – had recovered his balance with remarkable speed, darting forward and scooping up a g-Taser shaken from the grasp of one of her officers. What was surprising was that instead of pointing it in her direction, he had aimed it at the head of his young companion. It didn't make any sense.

Around her, Harrison and the rest of her security team were struggling to regain their feet, their own confusion etched on their faces as they stared at the two intruders. Sillitoe, the rookie assigned to her team on this tour, was cursing loudly as he pulled himself off the floor, blood trickling from a painful-looking gash on his forehead.

'What the hell happened, Captain? It felt as though the entire damn base was …' He broke off as he noticed the Doctor and Bill, and his hand immediately reached for the g-Taser at his belt. 'Son of a …'

'Steady, Sillitoe.' Laura placed a restraining hand on his arm. The wrong move at this juncture could result in things ending very badly. She frowned. There was something not quite right here.

As if reading her mind, the Doctor gave a thin smile and shifted his hold on the butt of the pistol, moving his thumb to reveal a small red warning light glowing steadily on the grip. Laura's heart sank.

'I'm certain that you know what that light means,' called the Doctor.

Laura nodded. 'I'm well aware of its significance. Are you?'

'Oh, yes.'

'Well, will someone please tell *me*?' Bill's voice was shrill and strained. Whatever was going on here, the girl was as surprised by it as everyone else.

'This is a gravity-Taser,' explained the Doctor, calmly. 'It's a variation on the standard sidearm used on the majority of spacecraft and off-world facilities throughout the Terran empire. No projectile weapons allowed, you see. Bullets and pressurised environments don't tend to go well together. The same goes for high-energy weapons. But this …' The Doctor waggled the pistol. 'Very clever.

Emits a gravity pulse capable of knocking someone off their feet, or rendering them unconscious, with no threat of damaging any important structures or equipment.'

He paused.

'But with the safety cut-out disengaged, and at this close range …'

'Then the gravity pulse will take her goddamn head off!' Sillitoe finished the sentence for him.

Laura shook her head in despair. When this was over, she would have to give the rookie a good talking to about the use of tact in a hostage situation.

'Doctor?' Bill was now looking extremely frightened. 'Will you *please* tell me what you are doing?'

The Doctor shrugged. 'Well I can hardly threaten *them*, can I?' He nodded towards Laura and her officers. 'I've just spent the last ten minutes trying to convince them that I mean them no harm, so it's not going to look very good if I then go waving a gun in their faces, is it? I could threaten to shoot myself, I suppose – I've tried that before with reasonable success – but it's me! I can't go around shooting me. I'm brilliant! I'd never be able to forgive myself. So the only option is you.'

'And how is threatening to shoot me going to help our situation?' Bill's voice was now little more than a squeak.

'Ah, well now …'

Laura was certain that she saw the Doctor give his companion the smallest of winks.

Manoeuvring himself so that he was standing directly behind Bill, the Doctor glanced up at the hovering security orbs. 'Our metal friends here are an incredibly complicated piece of positronic engineering. They have to be, don't they? Putting law enforcement into the hands of an artificial intelligence is potentially extremely dangerous. Which means that you have to have layer upon layer of safety protocols, ensuring that their one overriding concern is to protect the innocent.'

He smiled at the orbs.

'So, fellas, you have to ask yourself, who is the innocent party here? It's not me, obviously. I was caught red-handed with a diamond in my pocket, and I've got a gun. Oh, yeah, I'm a bad boy! But Miss Potts here, she's not been accused of anything yet, she's not been found with incriminating evidence, she's not been questioned as to how she came to be here, and she's the one being threatened by a madman with a gun.'

The Doctor paused for a moment, the smile still playing around his lips.

'But who is she *really* in danger from, eh? Looking at all the available evidence you'd have to deduce that we arrived together, so we obviously know each other. She's made no attempt to escape from me, on the contrary, the first chance she had, she tried to make it make to my side, and so you'd have to conclude that we are friends. Now, do you think that if she's my friend, I'm really going to shoot her? No, of course not! Well … I say of course not. I have actually shot a friend once. But there were extenuating circumstances. And it was on Gallifrey. And he got better. But what about them …?'

He pointed at Laura and her officers.

'Just *look* at them. I mean, no offence, but one or two of them don't exactly look the sharpest knives in the drawer. Dedicated to their duty, of course, but fallible. Emotional. Human. Now, what would be the most likely outcome if they tried to rush me, or tried to shoot me? The probability is that my finger would tighten on the trigger, my own gun would fire and there would be a casualty. An *innocent* casualty. So, using your cold deductive logic, who here is the most immediate danger to Miss Potts? Is it me?'

He shrugged.

'Or is it them?'

The spheres hung motionless for a moment, processors clicking softly inside their gleaming metal shells then, with a blur of speed, they swept towards the startled security officers, whip-like probes cracking as they disabled each of their g-Tasers.

'That's better.' The Doctor was grinning broadly now. 'Now, shall we go and find someone in charge? From the shake we were given earlier, I think that this facility has rather more to worry about than me making off with one of your diamonds. In fact, I have a sneaking suspicion that you're going to be very glad that I'm here.'

Herded by the security orbs, Laura followed her officers towards the service lift, the expression on Sillitoe's face leaving no doubt as to what he felt about the situation. The Doctor brought up the rear, the g-Taser still pointed at the Bill's head. As they approached the lift, Laura was pleased to see her kick the Doctor hard in the shins.

'I really hate you sometimes,' Bill whispered.

Delitsky paced around the hangar for what felt like the thousandth time, trying desperately to make sense of things in his head. What had just happened should not have been possible, and yet, there was the mining pod, defiantly, *impossibly* empty.

In the shadows around the walls of the hangar, clusters of technicians huddled together, talking in hushed, frightened tones. Delitsky knew that he had to keep some order amongst his team, but it was going to be a tricky task. How do you expect people to act rationally when what they have just witnessed is completely irrational?

Through the observation window above him he could see Nettleman and Rince shouting and screaming at anyone and everyone who came near them. He wasn't sure what they were more upset about, the loss of the diamonds or the loss of the crewmember.

He shook his head. No. Sadly he knew *exactly* which of those two they were more upset about. The one blessing was that communications were being severely disrupted by the violence of the storm that still raged below them, so head office didn't know about the accident for the moment.

Delitsky just wished he knew what he was going to tell them.

'Delitsky …' Teske emerged from the hatch of the mining bell. From her expression she was even more confused than he was. 'I've run bio-scanners over every inch of the interior. If there had been a pressure breach, there would be some DNA evidence, and besides there would still be …'

'The pressure armour, yeah, I know, I know.' Delitsky already knew that asking for the scan was a waste of time. He just felt that he had to do something. He turned to his medical officer with a sigh. Having exhausted all the rational explanations, they had no other choice than to turn to the impossible ones. 'So, that last communication from Baines …'

'That there was something outside the pod? Jorgen, if you put that in your report, they'll commit both of us.'

'Then where the hell did he go, Johanna? Where the hell did he—'

A sudden commotion in the control room above caught Delitsky's eye. A large group of people had entered the mine-head, security officer Palmer amongst them. At the rear of the group he could see a tall man and a girl he didn't recognise …

'Who are those two?' Teske had spotted the strangers too. Her eyes widened. 'Jorgen, he's got a gun!'

All the tension that had been building in Delitsky erupted into anger. The first accident in fifteen years, a man overboard and now this?

Ignoring Teske's urging to slow down, he stormed across the hangar, bounding up the metal staircase taking the steps two at a time. At least this problem was real, tangible, something he could understand and confront.

'Pirates?' he growled. 'Not on *my* rig!'

Laura watched in dismay as Rig Chief Delitsky burst into the control room with a face like thunder.

'Will someone kindly explain to me what the devil is going on!' he bellowed.

She approached Delitsky slowly, her hands raised in an effort to calm him. 'Chief, we have a situation here ...'

'A situation?' Delitsky hissed. 'You're telling me we have a situation. There are six of you, six highly trained security officers who I am told are best the Federation has to offer, plus those ... ball bearings, and you get overpowered by a teenage girl and a pensioner?'

Palmer winced, this really was not how she'd wanted this tour of duty to start. 'It's not as straightforward as it looks, Chief ...'

'I'll tell you exactly how it looks, Captain Palmer, it looks like incompetence, it looks like … Hey! You! Get away from those controls!'

Delitsky pushed past Palmer angrily. Whilst all eyes had been on the confrontation between the Rig Chief and his security officer, the Doctor had surreptitiously made his way to the main control bank and was studying the readouts intently.

'Hmm?' The Doctor looked up.

'I said, get away from those controls!'

There was a sharp intake of breath around the room as Delitsky took another step forward. The Doctor raised his gun arm, and then stared in surprise at the weapon in his hand, almost as if he had forgotten he was holding it.

'It's just that I think that you might be missing something.' He casually placed the g-Taser on top of the console and turned back to the screens. 'If you look at—'

Delitsky might have been disappointed with his security team, but he couldn't fault their responses now. Almost as soon as the weapon left the Doctor's fingers, he vanished under a mountain of bodies. Moments later he was pinned against the wall with his hands firmly held behind his back.

Satisfied that she had things back under her control, Captain Palmer turned to Delitsky apologetically. 'Chief, I can only—'

'You can save it for the official inquiry, Captain Palmer.'

Palmer groaned inwardly as Nettleman pushed forward, Rince hovering at his shoulder as always. Typical of both of them. Cowering behind the rest of the crew when there was the faintest hint of danger, but keen to assert their authority as soon as that danger had passed.

'Now, what is going on here, Captain?' Nettleman glared at Palmer doing his best to look ferocious.

'Yes,' piped up Rince. 'Who are these people? How did they get on board?'

Palmer did her best to disguise her contempt for them both, with only partial success. 'The man calls himself the Doctor, the girl's name is Bill.' Palmer deliberately paused for effect. 'We found them in the vault.'

'The vault?'

Palmer had to supress a smile as Nettleman's voice went up a whole octave.

'The diamonds …' he squeaked.

'Are perfectly safe.' Palmer held out the stone that she had found in the Doctor's pocket. 'We recovered this one from the man.'

Nettleman snatched it from her in horrified indignation. 'How did they breach security?'

'We'll need to review data.'

'You'll need to do more than that, Captain. This is an unacceptable—'

'That's enough!' Delitsky's voice cut Nettleman dead. 'We can argue about who or what is at fault later. In the meantime, can I remind you that we have a slightly more immediate situation to deal with, so will everyone who isn't directly needed please get the hell out of my control room!'

Yes, Chief.' Palmer nodded, grateful for his intervention. She'd no doubt get the sharp end of his tongue later, but at least it wouldn't be in front of the entire crew. She turned to the officers holding the Doctor and Bill. 'You heard the Chief, get them out of here. Lock them both in the brig, I'll question them later.'

'I think that you'd actually be better off listening to what I have to say now, rather than later.' The Doctor's voice rang out across the control room.

Sillitoe cuffed him across the back of the head. 'Quiet, you.'

'Sillitoe,' snapped Palmer in irritation. 'That's enough, rookie!'

The Doctor shot a look in her direction, a look that gave her the strangest feeling of approval. 'As I was saying,' he continued, 'I can see that you're very busy people, and you've probably got lots of important meetings to have and memos to write and official reprimands to dish out, but you might want to check the high-frequency end of your emergency communications channel. Right now ...'

Delitsky gave a snort of contempt, his patience clearly at an end. 'I don't have time for this, just get him out of here!'

At a nod from Palmer, Sillitoe hauled the Doctor to his feet, pushing him towards the door.

'It's important,' the Doctor called over his shoulder. 'If you want to save a man's life!'

Hunched over his controls, Delitsky wasn't even listening to what he was saying any more.

On impulse, Palmer tapped the comms bud in her ear, scrolling through the frequencies to the emergency communication channel. Nothing. Except … There *was* something. Very faint. She boosted the volume.

And her jaw dropped.

'Chief, you need to hear this.'

Ignoring the puzzled looks that her officers were giving her, Palmer hurried to the communications console, adjusting the controls and opening the monitor channel. A faint, desperate voice echoed from the speakers.

'*Control … please … help. Control …. Can you hear …? Control …*'

Johanna Teske stared at Delitsky in disbelief.

'That's … That's Baines …'

Chapter

6

Bill could only marvel at how the Doctor could take an impossible, hopeless, *ridiculously* one-sided situation and somehow turn it to his advantage. Despite the fact that he'd been caught red-handed nicking a diamond from a vault, despite the fact that he'd disarmed and embarrassed an entire squad of security officers, despite the fact that he'd pointed a loaded gun at her head (and she'd be having words with him about *that!*), he had somehow come out on top – not quite the hero of the hour, there was still too much distrust about who he was and where he had come from for that – but certainly with more respect than he had commanded a few scant minutes ago.

All around her the control room was a maelstrom of frantic activity as the crew slipped into what was obviously a well-rehearsed set of emergency procedures. Unsurprisingly the Doctor was right in the middle of it, sitting at the scanner controls with a young lady named Claire Robbins helping to pinpoint exactly where the lost crewmember was in the atmosphere below. Delitsky was watching every move he made like a hawk. The crew might be grateful to the Doctor for finding their missing shipmate, but that didn't mean they totally trusted him. Out of the corner of her eye, Bill could see Officer Sillitoe watching him balefully from his post by the main door. There was someone who was definitely going to bear a grudge.

Suddenly feeling superfluous to proceedings, Bill slumped back in her chair, wincing at the pain from her elbow as she did so. She shrugged out of her denim jacket, rolling up her sleeve and grimacing at the livid bruise that was starting to form. She had thumped it harder than she had thought in the vault, and it was already starting to stiffen up.

'Are you hurt?'

Bill looked up to see a middle-aged woman with shoulder-length brown hair looking down at her, a concerned frown creasing her brow. From her uniform she was a medic of some kind. Bill shrugged. 'Just a bruise. Argument with a wall.'

'Well, I'm a bit of a spare wheel here until they locate Baines. Let me see what I can do.' The woman sat down, opening up a compact medical kit. 'Bill, was it?'

Bill nodded. 'That's right.'

'I'm Johanna.' She extended a hand. 'Call me Jo.'

Bill shook her hand, grateful for a friendly face, and for someone who could help her make sense of things. 'Thanks.'

Taking hold of Bill's arm, Johanna began gently probing the bruised flesh with experienced fingers. 'Your friend the Doctor knows how to make an entrance.'

'Yeah, he knows how to find trouble as well.' Bill winced as the medic touched a particularly sore spot.

'You're not wrong there. Still, if Baines gets out of this in one piece then it's going to go a long way to helping your case.'

'Our case?'

Johanna gave her a stern look. 'You were caught red-handed stealing diamonds from the vault, remember?'

'Oh.' Bill looked sheepish. 'Yeah, that.' She changed the subject. 'So, this crewman you've lost overboard ...'

'Baines.'

'Yeah, Baines. How is it that he's still alive? I mean that's Saturn out there. I'm no scientist, but shouldn't he have been crushed, or fallen towards the centre of the planet or something?'

'You can thank Jenloz and his team for that.' Johanna nodded at the short man in the boiler suit hunched over one of the consoles in the centre of the control room. 'They're responsible for all the anti-gravity engineering on this rig. Without them, we wouldn't even be here. Baines is wearing anti-gravity pressure armour, sort of like a survival suit, and as long as that's working ...'

Bill frowned, peering through the control room window at the squat spherical shape of the mining pod. 'But shouldn't he have been in that thing? It doesn't look like something you could fall out of easily …'

Johanna said nothing, concentrating instead on applying a clear gel of some kind to Bill's arm. You didn't have to be a genius to realise that something unusual had happened, something that the medic was not in the mood to discuss. She screwed the lid back onto the tube of gel, dropping it back into her medical kit. 'That should help with the swelling. You'll be sore for a couple of hours, but there's no serious harm done.'

'Thanks.' Bill rubbed her arm. Amazingly the bruise was already started to fade. 'You know, if there's some kind of trouble here, I mean trouble *other* than the fact that you've lost a man overboard, then the Doctor can probably help.'

Johanna regarded her carefully for a moment, then took a deep breath, obviously wanting to say something. Before she could do so, angry voices erupted from the far side of the control room. One of those voices was all too familiar.

The Doctor.

Bill rolled her eyes, 'Just hold that thought for a moment.'

Snatching up her jacket, Bill hurried over to where the Doctor and Delitsky were glowering at each other angrily. The Rig Chief was practically purple with rage and, given the supercilious expression on the Doctor's face, it didn't need much imagination on her part to work out what had gone on. The Doctor really did have an uncanny knack of rubbing people up the wrong way.

'Making friends, are we?' asked Bill, raising an eyebrow at him pointedly.

The Doctor turned and glared at her. 'Will you please tell this pudding brain to stop arguing with me and let me do what I do best!'

'And what is that, exactly? Apart from telling everyone how much cleverer than them you are?'

'That's exactly my point!' yelled the Doctor. Pushing past Delitsky he strode across to a console, swiping at the controls and bringing up a display on a monitor screen. 'That –' he pointed a bony finger at a faintly pulsing red blob on the centre of the screen – 'is your missing crewman. He's suspended in a gravity null point a kilometre below this station. The generators in his armour are working at maximum capacity, which gives him another nineteen and a half minutes before the batteries are exhausted and he's dragged into the centre of the planet. That's nineteen and a half minutes when we need to stop discussing things in committee and *do* something!'

'And I'm telling you that there is nothing we *can* do!' bellowed Delitsky. 'He is too far into the planet's atmosphere for us to mount any kind of meaningful rescue attempt and I'm not prepared to risk the lives of any more of my crew—'

'You don't have to risk anyone!' the Doctor interrupted. 'I can rescue him on my own. Me!' He turned to Bill in frustration. 'Tell him! Just tell him!'

'Tell him?' Bill frowned. 'Tell him what?'

'About the TARDIS!'

'Oh!'

That came as something of a surprise. She had assumed that the Doctor would want to keep the TARDIS a secret. The fact that he didn't … Bill suddenly realised just how urgent the situation was becoming.

'Right, the TARDIS … Well …' She paused for a moment, unsure of exactly how best to describe it. 'It's kind of a spacecraft, only it's not. It's a box, quite a tatty-looking box, but that's just a disguise, inside it's all "ooooh" and "aaaaah", like a super-swanky kitchen …'

Out of the corner of her eye, she could see the Doctor shaking his head in despair. Delitsky was just staring at her as if she was mad.

She felt her face flushing with embarrassment. 'Well, it's not that easy to explain …'

'This is ridiculous,' snarled Delitsky. 'Why I ever agreed to let you—'

'Wait!' The Doctor suddenly clapped his hands together, spinning on his heel. 'I've got it!'

He hurried across the control room to where Jenloz and his team of engineers were watching him in astonishment. Bill groaned. As always, when the Doctor ran anywhere he looked ridiculous. 'A penguin with its arse on fire,' she muttered under her breath.

The Doctor crouched down, bringing his head level with that of the diminutive Chief Engineer. 'I'm guessing that you're the one with the real brains around here, yes? I mean it only stands to reason, it's you and your guys who do all the hard work on this rig, all the gravity calculations, the maintenance. Everyone else in this control room just seems to do a lot of shouting. And in order to properly calibrate the gravity inverters you must have sensors everywhere, inside and out. Am I right?'

Jenloz just nodded.

'Even in the vault?'

'Captain Palmer!' Delitsky's patience was finally at an end. ' Get this lunatic out of here!'

As security officers advanced on the Doctor once more, he backed away from the little engineer, his eyes pleading. 'Just turn on your gravity sensors in the vault and tell them what you see. Please.'

The security men loomed over him. Bill could see Officer Sillitoe's lip curling into an unpleasant sneer. He grasped the Doctor roughly by the arms. 'Right, sunshine, I think we've just about had enough of you.'

'Stop!' Jenloz was staring at the readouts scrolling across his screen in disbelief. Hopping from his chair, he scurried over to Delitsky.

'Chief, whatever it is that's sitting up there in the vault we need to get it down here. Right now.'

The Doctor caught Bill's eye, and just smiled.

Laura watched as the activity in the control room reached fever pitch. Her admiration for the engineering crew had just gone up a notch. It had seemingly been the work of moments for Jenloz and his team to get the Doctor's box moved down from the vault, manoeuvring it through service hatches and lift shafts by means of a series of sophisticated robotic cargo movers.

Now it was in the hangar, incongruously sitting in the spot previously occupied by the mining pod, a swarm of technicians bustling around it as they struggled to attach it to the mining winches. Laura couldn't possibly imagine how this ridiculous-looking contraption was going to help rescue Baines, but Jenloz was adamant that this 'TARDIS' was exactly what they needed.

The little Cancri engineer was chattering excitedly to Delitsky. She had rarely seen him so animated. Whatever readings he had got from that box, it had convinced him that the Doctor was the solution to this crisis.

The Doctor himself was standing to one side, arguing with Johanna Teske as she attempted to persuade him to wear the various medical sensors that she had produced. His young girl companion, Bill was hovering at his shoulder.

'Is this really a good idea, Captain?'

Lynne Harrison sounded nervous. Laura gave a deep sigh. Her sergeant was only saying out loud what she was thinking herself. They didn't know who this man was, where he had come from or how he had got here, they'd caught him in the act of taking a diamond from the vault, and yet …

Laura stared at the lanky figure in the hangar below as he finally gave up in his attempts to dissuade Teske from wiring him up, and reluctantly allowed her to start attaching sensors to his forehead and torso. If this strange blue box of his really was a spacecraft of some kind then he had had ample opportunity to escape with his friend, either when they were still in the vault, or as they had made their way down to the control room.

No, his entire manner had changed as soon as he had realised that there was some kind of problem on board the mine, and especially once he had become aware that there was a life in danger. Laura might not know anything about this strange man, but her gut instinct told her that they could trust him.

'Let's just wait and see how things go, shall we, Sergeant?'

Harrison shrugged. 'Your call, Captain, but you've got some pretty high-powered bigwigs looking over your shoulder if things go belly up.' She nodded towards the far side of the control room.

Laura followed her gaze. Nettleman and Rince were also watching the preparations in the hangar. Harrison was right. The two Kollo-Zarnista executives were looking far from happy at the gamble that she and Delitsky were taking. If this didn't end with the safe return of Baines, then this might be the last trip to Saturn that she ever made.

'I don't understand why you're allowing this, Nettleman.' Clive Rince chewed on the arm of his glasses nervously. 'We don't know anything about those two ...'

Donald Nettleman didn't take his eyes off the Doctor. 'This "Doctor" and his friend could be exactly what we've been waiting for.'

'But he managed to get into the vault!' hissed Rince.

'Yes, and I'd really like to learn how he did that, but for the moment, I want to let Delitsky play his hand.'

'But ...'

'The situation is already a mess, Rince ...' From the tone of his voice, Nettleman was in no mood to waste time discussing this. 'Head office is bound to send more people now, regardless of whether they manage to rescue that miner or not. But at the moment Delitsky and the others have their hands full. Which reminds me ...'

He reached into his jacket pocket, pulling out the diamond that had been recovered from the Doctor.

'You had better give this back to Captain Palmer and get one of her team to return it the vault.'

He pushed it into Rince's hand.

'We don't want to be accused of stealing, now, do we?'

* * *

'Right, That's the last one.' Johanna Teske pressed the final sensor pad onto the Doctor's temple and nodded with satisfaction.

'Is all this really necessary?' sighed the Doctor, scratching at the self-adhesive pads dotted across his forehead.

'Yes. I want to be able to monitor your vital signs at every stage. I've lost one man today – I'm not going to lose another.'

The Doctor opened his mouth to make some pithy remark, then thought better of it.

Jo picked up her medical bag. 'I'd better get back to my console, make sure the readings are coming through OK.' She paused. 'Doctor, if you ... see anything when you're down there ...' She tailed off.

'See anything?' The Doctor raised an eyebrow.

The medic shook her head, suddenly looking embarrassed. 'Nothing. Forget it. Just be careful.'

The Doctor watched as she made her way across the hangar. 'I wonder what was that about?'

'I dunno.' Bill shrugged. 'But at least they're trying to look after you.' She was looking worried. 'Can I *please* come with you?'

The Doctor shook his head. 'No. I'm going to be taking enough risks, as it is. Don't want any distractions.'

'Thanks a lot!'

'Listen,' barked the Doctor. 'This is going to be tricky, even for me.'

'Well then, I can help.'

'No!' His tone softened, ever so slightly. 'Look, I can't do this and be worrying about you as well ...'

'OK.' That was as close an admission as Bill was going to get that he was actually taking her into consideration at all. It still didn't quite make up for the fact that he had pointed a gun at her head, but it would do. For the moment.

She glanced at the huge clamps that the technicians had attached to the TARDIS roof, and the massive winches that loomed in each corner of the hangar.

'So, is all this palaver really necessary? Couldn't you just, you know, *fly* the TARDIS down there?'

The Doctor gave her the same despairing look that he always did when she asked a stupid question in one of his classes. 'Miss Potts, do you really think that I'd be going to all this trouble if I could?'

'Why not? You're the one who keeps telling me how amazing the TARDIS is.'

'And if you've got a spare hour or two for me to lecture you on the specifics of extreme gravitational stresses created by gas giants, and the effects that those stresses can cause in relation to short-duration navigation through interstitial time when materialising within a gravity compensation field then I'll be happy to go through the figures, but given that we've got less than –' he glanced at his watch – 'seven minutes before Mr Baines becomes a permanent part of the atmosphere of Saturn, I think that we'd better stick to the current plan, yes?'

Bill nodded sheepishly. 'Right.'

'Actually, I think I might want to come to that lecture as well ...' The engineer, Jenloz, was waiting expectantly. 'We're ready to depressurise the hangar, Doctor.'

The Doctor nodded. 'Can you do me a favour and make sure Bill is looked after whilst I'm gone? Preferably somewhere well out of reach of that security thug, Sillitoe.'

'Of course.' The little Cancri nodded enthusiastically. Ever since he had lain eyes on the gravity sensor readings that the TARDIS was giving off – he had become something of a fanboy. He wasn't kidding about wanting to listen to the Doctor give a lecture. He'd probably want a guided tour of the TARDIS as well.

A klaxon started to blare, and Delitsky's voice boomed around the hangar. '*All crew, please take your stations. Hangar depressurisation countdown commencing in one minute. Doctor, you'd better get ready.*'

All around, technicians hurried to clear the room. Catching hold of Bill's arm, Jenloz steered her towards the stairwell, snatching one quick glance over his shoulder as he went, hoping to catch a glimpse of the inside of the TARDIS.

The Doctor rolled his eyes. Just what he needed. A gravity nerd.

He watched as Bill climbed the stairs towards the control room, catching her eye and giving her a reassuring nod. Then he turned and unlocked the TARDIS.

Delitsky watched as the Doctor vanished inside the ridiculous blue box and the rickety door closed behind him. He couldn't actually believe that they were going through with this, but if what Jenloz had told him was to be believed (and Delitsky had learned over the years to trust everything that his engineer told him) then that blue box was a masterpiece of gravitic engineering.

Focusing on the task in hand, the Rig Chief started the countdown. 'All crew. Stand by to initiate rescue drop.'

He suddenly heard a sharp intake of breath from the metical station. He looked across to see Johanna Teske staring open-mouthed at her screen as the Doctor's bio-readings started to come through.

'Problem?'

Teske tore her eyes from the monitor screen and stared at him for a second, then shook her head. 'No. No, we're good.'

'Right then.' Delitsky turned back to the task in hand. 'Doctor. Stand by. We're initiating drop in … Five. Four. Three. Two. One. Drop.'

In a swirl of boiling vapour the TARDIS vanished through the hatch in the floor.

Chapter

7

The small blue box fell through the clouds of Saturn, an insignificant speck against the swirling splendour of the gas giant. Gravitational forces capable of crushing the mightiest starships to dust tore at the seemingly flimsy shell, but the workers in the timeshipyards of Gallifrey had done too good a job. Almost as if frustrated by this perversion of the laws of nature, a huge storm began to rage in the planet's atmosphere.

Inside, the Doctor clung to the central control column of the TARDIS as the time machine jerked and rolled. On the screen jutting from the panel in front of him, he watched as the huge, hulking shape of the mine raced away from him before vanishing from view, swallowed up by the roiling clouds.

For the first time in millennia, the Doctor took a moment to check on the status of the TARDIS's gravitic anomaliser, suddenly conscious of just how important it was in stopping him being crushed to the size of a grain of salt.

'*Doctor, this is Delitsky.*' The Rig Chief's voice crackled from a grill in the console, distorted by the gravity waves flowing around the TARDIS. '*Baines is still showing as being directly below you, you're coming up on him fast.*'

The Doctor stabbed at a control, changing the view on the screen to a schematic that showed his approach to the stranded crewman. A numeric readout was scrolling down at frightening speed. Six hundred metres, five hundred metres, four hundred metres …

'*We're going to bring you to a halt at ten metres. That's a close as we dare. After that, it's up to you.*'

'Oh, the difficult bit you mean,' muttered the Doctor through gritted teeth as the storm buffeted the TARDIS like a toddler shaking a rattle.

On the screen, the rapidly descending countdown started to slow until, with a sudden jolt, the TARDIS came to a halt. Scurrying around the console, the Doctor started to make delicate adjustments to the controls. Extending the force field to create a stable corridor from the main doors was something that he had done on many occasions, but never in quite as hostile an environment as the one that he now found himself in. Satisfied that the settings were correct, the Doctor slipped on his sonic sunglasses, and operated the door control.

The TARDIS control room was immediately bathed in a harsh yellow light. The Doctor strode across to the door and stared out at the apocalyptic view. Thick, choking clouds swept past the TARDIS at terrifying speed, spitting, sparking balls of energy bursting into existence as the powerful envelope of the force field deflected the streams of gas. Lightning bolts arced in huge zigzag lines across the sky, revealing a monstrous, boiling cloudscape that seemingly stretched off to infinity. And amongst it all, glinting with each blinding flash of electric blue light, diamonds fell like rain, streaming off the force field and falling in sparkling streams towards the planet's core far, far below.

The Doctor had seen many wondrous sights during his travels, but this was enough for even him to stop for a moment and stare in admiration and respect at the power on display. It seemed inconceivable that something as fragile as a human being could survive alone amongst all this chaos.

Reminded of the reason why he was here, the Doctor activated his sonic sunglasses, using the interface with his optic nerve to initiate a scan for the missing miner. Immediately there was a contact. The Doctor blinked twice, enhancing and zooming the image.

Hanging in the maelstrom was a figure, tiny and insignificant against the majesty of Saturn. The Cancri-designed pressure armour looked ugly and uncomfortable, as if someone had blended a suit of medieval armour with a diving bell, but it had done its job keeping its occupant alive. With the enhanced view afforded by his glasses, the Doctor could see the twisting, spiralling energies of the gravity inverters as they fought against the immense pull of the planet below. Gravity nerd he might be, but the Doctor had to admit that Jenloz and his species were pretty impressive engineers.

Interfacing with the TARDIS console via his glasses, the Doctor concentrated, narrowing and stretching the force field until it encompassed the motionless figure. Lightning cracked explosively around him and he hurried along the invisible corridor until he reached the stricken miner.

'Baines?' The Doctor tried to peer into the suit, but there was no visor, no way of seeing inside the thick armour. 'Can you hear me in there?' The Doctor rapped his knuckles on the metal torso. 'Baines!'

Desperately hoping that he hadn't arrived too late, the Doctor started to unbuckle his belt. The gravity inverters meant that the suit was floating like some bizarre novelty helium balloon. He just needed to tow it back to the TARDIS.

As he fumbled with his buckle, he suddenly became aware of movement out of the corner of his eye, and turned in time to see a vast dark shadow slide across the crackling surface of the force field, moving like oil over water.

Startled, he stumbled backwards, an involuntary cry of surprise bursting from his lips as the shape shot past him. He spun around, trying to catch a better glimpse of whatever the thing was, but there was nothing – nothing but swirling gas and jagged lightning.

He swiftly adjusted the settings on his sonic sunglasses, cycling through dozens of different scanning options. He leaned forward. There. Right at the extreme edge of his vision, a dark smudge. A smudge that was moving in the *opposite* direction to the rest of the clouds … As the Doctor struggled get a firm reading from the strange phenomena, an alarm started to sound on Baines' suit.

The Doctor cursed in Gallifreyan under his breath. He was out of time.

Tearing himself away from the mysterious object in the clouds, the Doctor hurried across to the miner, fastening the buckle of his belt onto a hook on the front of the armoured suit. He hoped that he hadn't left things too late. The suit was already beginning to float lower than it had done previously, and the strange green glow from the Cancri gravity inverters was beginning to fade rapidly. If they failed completely, the Doctor wasn't sure that he would be able move Baines in his own.

Wrapping the belt around his fist, the Doctor started to haul the miner back along the force-field corridor towards the TARDIS. Through the open doors he could hear Delitsky's frantic voice on the speaker.

'Doctor! Are you there? Doctor!'

Ignoring the insistent voice, the Doctor hauled Baines into the TARDIS. The suit crashed against the doorframe, and for one horrible second he realised that he'd not worked out if he could actually get the bulky armour through the doors or not.

Grasping Baines by the shoulders, the Doctor heaved with all his might. There was a horrible splintering noise as the pressure armour scraped through the gap. At the same moment there was a 'pop' and the gravity inverters finally shut down.

The suit hit the ground with a deafening crash, the impact sending the Doctor skidding across the floor of the TARDIS. He scrambled to his feet and darted to the central console, reaching out for the door control. As his hand touched the lever, he was suddenly aware of a dark shape flashing past the open doorway, making the edges of the force field pop and spark like embers in a fire.

His eyes never leaving the doorway, the Doctor pulled the lever, closing the doors and shutting out the raging storm. And whatever else was out there.

'What the hell is going on down there? Our instruments are going crazy!'

The Doctor ignored the question. 'I've got Baines. You can bring us up.'

Bill craned her neck to try and get a better view of what was going on, but there were simply too many people crowded into the control room.

The TARDIS had reappeared in the hangar a few moments ago, the huge winches slowly spinning to a halt, and the heavy airlock doors shutting out the raging winds of Saturn with a clang that had made her ears ring.

Seconds later, the hangar depressurised and, to Bill's huge relief, the Doctor's tousled head peered out through the police box doors.

'Are you all just going to stand there and gawp, or is someone going to give me a hand with him?'

Bill hopped out of the way as Delitsky, Jo Teske and a tide of engineers surged into the hangar. Bill slipped in behind them, watching as the crew helped the Doctor to manhandle what looked like a massive metal diving suit out of the TARDIS and onto a complicated-looking gurney. Jo and Jenloz started connecting a bewildering array of equipment to sockets hidden beneath flaps on the suit's surface.

'Is he alive?' Concern was etched onto the Rig Chief's face.

Jenloz nodded. 'We're getting life readings.' He tapped a monitor screen with a stubby finger.

'Yeah, but I don't like those readings.' Jo looked even more anxious than the Chief. 'We need to get him stabilised and up to the med-bay, pronto.'

Bill made her way through the crowd of technicians to the Doctor's side. 'Are you OK?'

'Bit busy at the moment.' The Doctor pushed past her, helping Jo with another connection.

A bit hurt by his abruptness, Bill opened her mouth to complain, then realised how selfish she was being. He was trying to save a man's life.

She was suddenly barged out of the way by someone behind her. Furious, she turned to see the company suit, Nettleman, and his creepy little associate, Rince. Whilst she would put up with some rudeness on the part of the Doctor, she certainly wasn't going to take any nonsense from them.

'Hey, watch who you're shoving!'

The two men ignored her.

'Dr Teske,' snapped Nettleman. 'I need this man conscious so he can tell us what happened down there.'

The medic didn't look up. 'This man is in no condition to say anything to anyone at the moment.'

'I'm afraid that I have to insist.'

Jo Teske looked up angrily. 'You can insist as much as you like, Mr Nettleman, but it isn't going to make a blind bit of difference. This man has just spent twenty minutes floating in free orbit outside this rig. That is an unprecedented occurrence in nearly fifteen years of continuous operation. I have no idea what he has been exposed to, I have no idea what side effects we can expect, so I am taking him to the medical bay for further examination. Now, if you have some previously undeclared medical experience that you can bring to this situation then please do tell me, if not then stop wasting my time!'

Bill's admiration for the medical officer went up by several hundred per cent. Nettleman couldn't have looked more surprised if Jo had slapped him in the face with a wet fish. Even the Doctor looked taken aback. The crew, Delitsky included, made no attempt to hide their amusement and approval at the second smack-down that Nettleman had received. The man was definitely not popular.

Without giving him another moment of her attention, Jo turned and started to push the gurney across the hangar towards the lift.

Nettleman rounded on Delitsky practically shaking with rage. 'All right, Chief Delitsky. I have had enough of this insubordination. I want to see you, your senior engineer and your chief security officer in the meeting room, right now.'

With that, Nettleman started to push his way roughly through the crowd of suddenly sombre technicians and engineers. Rince followed in his wake.

'All right, people.' Delitsky gave a weary sigh. 'Let's start trying to get things back to normal here.'

As the crew started to disperse back to their usual stations, the Doctor caught Bill's eye, indicating that they should make use of the moment to follow Dr Teske. Bill nodded, and the two of them hurried towards the service lift.

As the lift doors closed, Bill caught a glimpse of Delitsky's drawn and haggard face. She didn't envy him the meeting he was about to have with Nettleman. She didn't envy him at all.

Nestled in the middle of the mining platform, the med-bay was small, well equipped and – after the noise and bustle of the control room – refreshingly calm and quiet. One corner of it was dominated by a huge gleaming cylinder, the words 'DEPRESSURISATION CHAMBER' stencilled in red on its doors.

The Doctor helped Jo manoeuvre the gurney into an alcove set into the wall alongside the chamber, and it locked into place with a satisfying click. Immediately the medical mainframe took over all monitor and life-support functions, relaying readings to the dozens of monitor screens scattered around the room. A low, soft rhythmic beep filled the air, adding to the calming atmosphere. Jo hurried over to her desk, shrugging off the jacket of her duty uniform and slipping on the ubiquitous white coat worn by all medical professionals instead.

Standing at the Doctor's elbow, Bill peered curiously at the bulky armour lying incongruously on the starched white sheets. 'There's no visor.' She frowned. 'How does he see out?'

'He doesn't,' said the Doctor somewhat unhelpfully. 'This –' he rapped the metal with his knuckles – 'is designed to stop the occupant being crushed to a pulp by atmospheric pressure. A visor would be a weak spot.'

'The armour has an internal holographic Head's-Up Display,' explained Jo. 'Sensor readings from the mining bell and the rig are relayed to the miners by the control team.'

Bill frowned. 'So the miners just float around in these things plucking diamonds out of the air?'

'Not exactly. The mining is done from a semi-automated pressure bell, lowered from the rig the same way that we lowered your ... spacecraft. The armour is a backup system, a failsafe in case something goes wrong with the bell.'

'So why did he climb out of the bell?'

'I'm not certain he climbed out. He thought that ...' Jo hesitated.

'He thought that he heard something outside.' The Doctor completed her sentence.

Bill's eyes widened. 'Something dragged him out?'

Jo shrugged helplessly, obviously not knowing what to believe. 'Right before we lost contact with him, he was convinced he could hear something. Something moving on the hull. But he couldn't have. It's impossible, isn't it?' She looked at the Doctor questioningly. 'Surely it has to be a freak weather phenomenon, or some electric disturbance due to the storm.'

The Doctor just stared at her silently.

'Well, why not just open this thing up and ask him?' Bill returned her attention to the armoured figure slumped on the gurney.

Jo shook her head. 'Because we can't.'

'Why not?'

'Because Baines has operated a failsafe protocol.' It was the Doctor who answered the question once more. 'I'm guessing that there is a highly complex, and extremely robust, set of safeguards whereby the occupant of this armour can lock it down from the inside, ensuring that the environment within cannot be compromised.'

'That's right.' Jo nodded. 'It has to be released from the inside.'

'But why would he do that?' asked Bill in bemusement. 'Why trap himself inside his own suit?'

'Because he was scared.' The Doctor's face was grim. 'So scared of whatever was outside the bell that he did the only thing he could, and locked it out.'

Chapter

8

Delitsky closed his eyes and tried to keep his temper. Nettleman had been yelling at them for nearly quarter of an hour now. Satisfying as it had been to see Teske rip him a new one, it had only served to put the Kollo-Zarnista executive in a truly foul mood. Things weren't being helped by Rince, who egged him on like a schoolboy in the playground urging on a bully to go further and further.

'Do you have any idea how much money we have lost on this shift alone?' yelled Nettleman.

Delitsky knew exactly how much money. Rince had spelled it out often enough. 'I am well aware—'

'Nearly three million dollars,' said Rince, just to drive the point home. 'That's assuming we can get production back on track by the end of the day.'

'Three million dollars. Not to mention any compensation payments that Baines may ask for. Those figures are not going to look good for this rig, Chief Delitsky. Not for you, and not for the bonus payments for your crew.'

'This has been an unprecedented situation, but now that the rescue operation has been—'

'And that's another thing,' Nettleman interrupted. 'How the devil did a convicted diamond thief take charge of your rescue operation?'

'Um, he's not actually convicted,' Laura Palmer corrected him, and Delitsky winced.

'Oh, really Captain Palmer,' Nettleman sneered at her. 'You catch a man in the vault with one of our diamonds in his pocket and you don't think he's guilty? You think that he just found it and was putting it back, perhaps?'

'No, sir, I'm just saying—'

'How the hell did he get in there? In that ridiculous box of his, I suppose!'

'Actually, that's very possible,' piped up Jenloz, his shrill voice sounding almost cheerful. 'I've been doing some calculations, and if you look at the gravitic readings that I was getting from the box, and them compare them to—'

'I don't give a damn about your readings!' Nettleman exploded. 'All I care about is getting this rig mining again. Chief Delitsky, can you give me *any* good reason why you cannot resume mining operations immediately?'

For the briefest of moments Delitsky wondered if he should tell Nettleman about the conversation that he had had with Baines just before the accident, but the look on his boss's face left him in no doubt of what would happen if started talking about an unidentified 'something' in the atmosphere of Saturn. Far better to wait until he had had a chance to question Baines and work out exactly what had happened.

'We still need to evaluate damage to the primary mining bell, but we can have the secondary bell in place and calibrated within the hour.'

'Another hour?' Nettleman looked pained. There really was no pleasing the man.

'Approximately an hour, yes.'

'Then you'd better get on with it.' Nettleman waved his hands at them dismissively. 'Get out of here, all of you. I've got to prepare a report that explains this mess to head office.'

Holding back the urge to punch the man, Delitsky nodded, then rose from his seat and filed out of the room with Palmer and Jenloz.

As soon as the door to the meeting room closed behind them, Palmer turned to him with a grimace. 'Nice to see that he still has his open and approachable management style.'

'Yeah,' Delitsky grunted. 'But unfortunately he and Rince *are* the ones calling the shots at the moment, and they can make our lives very unpleasant if they want to, remember that.'

'Yes, Chief.'

Delitsky sighed. 'Look, Palmer, whilst I'm grateful to the Doctor for getting Baines back for us, Nettleman's right:

we've given him a really long leash without knowing a damned thing about him. See what you can find out from him, OK? Something, *anything* that will get those two off my back. Otherwise I'm going to have no choice other than to press some kind of charges.'

'On it, Chief.' Tucking her hair under her cap, Palmer hurried away.

Delitsky turned to the little Cancri standing alongside him. 'Come on Jenloz. Let's see if we can light a fire under the repair teams and try to get this place back to some kind of normality.'

Even as he said it, Delitsky had the strangest feeling that it would be a long time before things approached anything remotely resembling normal again.

Satisfied that Baines was as comfortable as he could be under the circumstances, Jo turned her attention to the Doctor, whose forehead was still dotted with the sensor pads that she had attached earlier.

'Come over here and I'll get those off for you.'

She led him across to her desk, pushing him into a chair and pulling out a bottle of rubbing alcohol.

'So, your bio-readings were … unusual.' Jo didn't make eye contact with him, concentrating instead on removing the small self-adhesive circles from his skin.

'Not unusual where I come from.'

'Ah …'

'Which isn't anywhere local, as you've correctly surmised.'

'And her?' Jo nodded towards Bill.

'Oh, no, she's just a plain old pudding brain, same as you.'

Bill stuck her tongue out at him.

'Right, and the two of you are just …?'

'Friends. Travelling together.'

'In an old box.'

'Yes.'

'Doctor …' Jo placed the bottle back onto the desk and stared straight into his eyes. 'Did *you* see anything? Down there. In the clouds. It's just that your adrenalin rates …'

'Yes,' said the Doctor calmly. 'I think that I did see something.'

'But what?' Jo's eyes were shining with a mixture excitement and horror. 'I mean it's impossible! For something to live in that atmosphere, at those pressures. It must be totally …'

'Alien?' The Doctor raised an unruly grey eyebrow.

Jo gave a short, nervous laugh. 'Well, more alien than you are …'

The two of them smiled at each other.

'Doctor …' Jo's voice dropped to a conspiratorial whisper. 'My sister, my older sister, did her medical training at the Bi-Al Foundation, a Centre for Alien Biomorphology in the asteroid belt. She was seconded to a Professor Marius. She told me loads of really crazy stories over the years, but one of those stories concerned a man called the Doctor, a space traveller who helped bring a virulent viral infection under control. You look nothing like the man that she describes, but …' She hesitated for a moment. 'Are you that man?'

The Doctor stared at her, suddenly transported back to another time, another life, to his battle with the Nucleus of the Swarm.* He could see the family resemblance to Marius's nurse, not just in her features, but also in the same earnest determination in her eyes. It would be so easy to tell her the truth, to say 'Yes, I'm the same man, but in a different body' and wait to see her reaction. So easy to ask how her sister was doing, to get back in touch with Professor Marius and tell him about all the adventures that he had shared with his robot dog. So easy to make a connection, to do something … human. So easy …

If this had been any previous incarnation then the Doctor might just have done it, but not this one. Ever since he had started his new life cycle, ever since Trenzalore, he found it harder and harder to make those connections. Easier to keep himself shut away. To keep himself isolated.

Besides, he had duties. He had made a vow.

'No.' He shook his head. 'No, I'm sorry, that wasn't me …' He shrugged. 'Seems like there are a lot of doctors in the universe.'

---

*See *Doctor Who and the Invisible Enemy*.

'Oh.' The disappointment took all the sparkle from Jo's eyes. For a second, the Doctor almost changed his mind, then a voice from the doorway destroyed the moment for ever.

'Dr Teske, Captain Palmer would like to see you and the ... er, other Doctor in her office.'

'Well, I don't particularly want to see her,' snapped the Doctor, unsure whether he was angry with himself or with Sergeant Harrison's interruption.

Jo laid a gentle hand on his forearm. 'If you want my opinion, it could be useful for you to have a few more allies on this rig, and believe me, Laura Palmer is someone that you want to have on your side.'

The Doctor considered this for a moment, then nodded, seeing the wisdom of what she was saying.

'What about me?' Bill had been watching the Doctor and Jo with interest from the far side of the room. 'Does she want to see me too?'

'There's no need, surely?' asked Jo. 'Besides, it would be a huge help for me if Bill could stay and keep an eye on Baines.'

Harrison frowned. 'Um, I don't know about that, Doc ...'

'Come on, Lynne. It's not like I've got an entire medical team to help. It's just me, remember?'

Lynne Harrison still didn't look convinced.

'Look, the Doctor just risked his life to save him,' Jo pointed out. 'Do you really think he'd go to all that trouble just so Bill could put him in danger again?'

Harrison shrugged. 'I guess not.'

'Good. That's settled, then.' Jo picked up a small black device about the size of a cell phone off her desk and handed it to Bill. 'Emergency alarm. Baines is being constantly monitored by the mainframe, but if anything happens that you're not happy about, use it.' She turned and smiled at the Doctor. 'You have to know when to trust people, don't you, Doctor?'

The Doctor was starting to like the station medic more and more. He shot an inquisitive glace across at Bill. 'Can you cope for five minutes without me?'

Bill glared at him. 'Sorry to deliver such a crushing blow to your ego, but yes!'

Stifling a grin, the Doctor followed Harrison and Jo from the medical bay. The Doctor was beginning to like his new companion more and more too.

On the surface of Mimas sat COM-RADE 561. The machine was just one of hundreds of similar machines scattered on moons and planets throughout the solar system, part of the Federation's subspace communications network.

As vital for the security as it was for interplanetary communications, the COMmunication Relay And Data Examination array sifted through the millions of messages that went back and forth between Earth and the dozens of bases, mines, fixed-orbit stations and transport ships working far from home. More than just machines, but not quite artificial intelligences, the COM-RADE devices had been designed to look for anything unusual in the information that they processed, anything that might pose a threat, either to Earth or to its dependents. Should they deem anything potentially dangerous or illegal, they had a priority link to the Federation Security Mainframe in Manhattan to report their findings.

The security protocols embedded in the AI of COM-RADE 561 were more rigorous still. It was part of a subset of monitoring devices specifically tasked to assist with the security of the five Kollo-Zarnista mines that were working on Saturn.

Usually the communications sent from the rig followed a clearly defined pattern, but today something was different. Under any other circumstances, the message currently being transmitted was unusual enough for COM-RADE 561 to raise the alarm and yet, when it tried to do so, it found that it was blocked by a set of rarely implemented official override codes.

Its positronic brain struggling to resolve the conflict between reporting what it knew to be an unauthorised short-range transmission and obeying a priority command override, COM-RADE 561 could only listen.

'*Ringbearer to Raptor. Acknowledge please.*'

'*Raptor here. What's going on there? You were meant to get in touch hours ago.*'

'I couldn't. There's been a situation.'

'What kind of situation?'

'An accident on the rig, one of the miners overboard.'

'Careless of them.'

'There's something else … two strangers, Caught in the vault.'

'In the vault? Who are they? Where did they come from?'

'We don't know.'

'Then find out!'

'I will.'

'If you're trying to wriggle out of this …'

'I'm not, I promise.'

'Good. Because life will get very difficult for you if you do try anything. Raptor out.'

Slumped in the chair next to the gurney, Bill was dreaming. She hadn't intended to drop off, but the events of the last few hours (or, to be strictly accurate, the events of the last few days) had finally caught up with her. The quiet warmth of the medical bay, combined with the steady, rhythmic beep of the medical computer had finally proved too much for her exhausted body as well as her overstretched mind.

Not that her dreams were restful ones. Everyday subconscious worries about paying bills and keeping to schedules, of finding something positive about a dead-end job, of facing up to the possibility of failure and rejection had been replaced with nightmares of more monstrous nature.

Quite literally.

Sinuous shapes with gnashing teeth writhed beneath crackling ice, robots with smiley faces reached out for her with grasping hands, alien war machines with harsh, grating voices slid through roaring flames, her friend Heather stared into her eyes, water pouring down her face …

And there, in the shadows, in the background, always watching her, was another alien. The Doctor, the time traveller, his brow creased, his intense gaze never leaving her, his expression never giving the slightest indication of what he might be thinking.

More than anything, it was the Doctor that she wanted to impress, for him to see past the girl who just served chips. Without the Doctor, she was trapped in a world that she now knew was just one amongst millions. Without the Doctor she was trapped in a school canteen, in Moira's flat, in her tiny bedroom with that car alarm that went off every blessed night …

Beep. Beep. Beep.

Bill's eyes fluttered open as she slowly roused herself from the nightmare she was having.

That blasted car alarm …

Beep. Beep. Beep.

She suddenly jerked upright. The noise she was hearing wasn't part of her dream. It was in the room.

She scrambled from her seat, staring in horror at the suit of armour lying on the bed alongside her. All over the metal body warning lights were flashing, and the urgent beeping was getting higher and higher in pitch.

'Oh, no.' Bill could have cried with frustration. 'Please, no.'

Desperate to find any reason for what might be happening she stared up at the monitor screen mounted on the wall above the gurney. Most of the information was way too technical for her to understand, but two words were only too clear.

'DEPRESSURISATION IMMINENT.'

Bill hit the emergency alarm.

Chapter

9

'An alien life form,' Laura Palmer repeated slowly. 'Living in the clouds of Saturn.'

If it had been anyone other than Johanna Teske sitting in front of her, Laura would have locked them away for wasting police time.

'Does Delitsky know about this?'

Jo nodded. 'He was on the comms channel with me when Baines ... When the accident happened.'

Laura was trying to work out which of the hundreds of urgent questions she was going to ask next when Dr Teske's emergency alarm went off. Jo snatched it from her belt, and she and the Doctor stared at each other.

'Baines ...'

Exploding from their chairs, the two of them hared from the room.

Swearing loudly, Laura struggled to extricate herself from behind her desk. She barged her way through the startled officers milling around the security station, bellowing for her sergeant. 'Harrison. Medical bay, now!'

The two officers emerged into a corridor bustling with miners and support staff getting ready for the next shift. Laura could see the gangly figures of the Doctor and Jo vanishing around the gentle curve of the passageway.

Yelling at the bemused crewmembers to get out of the way, Laura raced after them, Harrison right on her heels. They arrived at the medical bay moments after the two doctors. Teske was busy at her desk readout whilst the Doctor was hunched over Baines in his pressure suit. The high-pitched alarm ringing around the room indicated only bad news to Laura's ears.

'What happened?'

Bill shrugged helplessly. 'I don't know … I …'

'There's been a failure in pressure integrity.' Teske didn't look up from her console. 'I'm trying to compensate.'

'It won't work,' said the Doctor grimly. 'Someone has disabled the pressure regulator.'

'Sabotage? You've got to be kidding.' Laura hurried across to the gurney.

'Well, he didn't do this himself.' The Doctor pointed a bony figure at a small panel on the suit. A portion of the brightly painted armoured surface had been cleanly removed, and Laura could see several connections that had clearly been cut on the circuitry inside.

She reached for the communicator on her belt. 'I'll get Jenloz up here.'

'He'll be too late.' The Doctor was frowning. 'We'll have explosive decompression any moment.'

'The Doctor's right,' yelled Jo. 'These pressure levels … They're way too high!'

'Then we need to get everyone out of here.' Laura grabbed hold of the Doctor's arm. 'There's nothing you can do.'

The Doctor shook his arm free angrily. 'Of course there's something I can do.' He pulled a slim, pen-like device from his jacket pocket. 'Bill, there's an emergency oxygen kit on the wall behind you, bring it over here, quickly.'

Bill pulled the cylinder from the wall and hurried over to the Doctor's side. Snatching it from her, he started to dismantle the main valve with his device, the low warbling noise that it made blending discordantly with the now frantic beeping from the suit.

Realising that trying to dissuade the Doctor from his task was just wasting time, Laura turned to Harrison. 'Get everyone you can out of this corridor. Get them back behind the vacuum doors. If that suit blows, I want to be able to seal off this section.'

'On it.' Harrison turned and ran from the room.

'And tell Delitsky what's happening!' Laura yelled after her.

She glanced over to where the Doctor was hunched over the gurney. Despite the ever more urgent noise from the alarm, he seemed unnaturally calm. Sporadically he would call for Bill to go and grab him yet another piece of equipment, dismantling it with incredible speed, and fitting the salvaged components into the suit.

Laura hesitated for a second, wondering if she should just trust in the Doctor's ability to bring this situation under control. Something about the man did engender the most incredible feeling of trust. But Laura was a pragmatist. She had been trained to deal with likely probabilities. And the most likely probability at the moment was that the Doctor was not going to be able to stop this in time.

Alongside her, Johanna Teske was also watching the Doctor work, the strained look on her face betraying the same conflicting emotions. Catching hold of her sleeve, Laura started to steer her towards the exit.

'Time to go, Doc.'

'But …'

'I'm not arguing about this, Jo.'

As they made their way towards the door of the med-bay, Laura could see Bill watching them. Her expression was impossible to read. Fear? Anger? Disappointment?

What was clear was that she trusted the Doctor with her life. Laura just hoped that her trust was not misplaced. At that very moment, the alarm emanating from Baines's suit went up in pitch again, and Laura realised that they were out of time.

In the control room, Delitsky watched in satisfaction as his crew started the final procedures to get mining operations back on track. Jenloz and his crew had done a great job getting the secondary bell hooked up in record time and, in the hangar below, miners were starting to prep their pressure armour for what was going to be a long shift.

It had taken a lot of promises to the union foreman to agree the intensive work patterns that Nettleman had insisted on. A lot of bonus payments and a lot of shore leave. That was not going to sit well with the bigwigs at Kollo-Zarnista, and Nettleman had left Delitsky in no doubt as to who was going to carry the can for this.

He had left the two men in the capable hands of his chief executive, Jenny Flowers, ostensibly because he had to get on with running the mine, but mainly because he was probably going to punch Nettleman if he had to spend any more time in his presence, and that would end his career with the company real quick.

Delitsky felt a pang of guilt about leaving Jenny to deal with those two weasels, but the woman had been very clear about wanting more responsibility … He gave a snort. Be careful what you wish for …

An alert button started to flash on his console. Frowning he tapped at his ear bud. 'Delitsky.'

'Chief, it's Sergeant Harrison …'

From the tone of her voice she was not bringing him good news.

'What's happened now, Sergeant?'

As Harrison explained the situation in the med-bay to him, Delitsky's heart sank. Could this day get any worse? He hauled himself from his chair, scanning the room until he caught sight of the man he was after.

'Arcon!' He waved the big man over.

'What's up, Chief?' He was someone else always eager for more responsibility. Today was his lucky day too.

'I need you to take over here.'

The surprise on Arcon's face was almost comical.

'I'll explain later,' said Delitsky, pushing him down into the chair. 'For the moment, just keep everything moving here.'

Ignoring the curious glances from the rest of his control team, Delitsky hurried from the room, breaking into a run as soon as he was outside the doors. The corridor was bustling with people getting ready for the next shift but the sight of their Rig Chief running anywhere was unusual enough for miners and support staff alike to get well out of his way.

Ignoring the elevators, Delitsky made for the stairwell, hauling himself up the steep metal steps two or three at a time until he emerged panting in the corridor three floors above the control deck.

Catching his breath, he started to jog towards the medical bay, conscious as he approached of an insistent high-pitched beeping that got louder with every step. That didn't bode well.

A murmuring crowd blocked the corridor ahead of him, and Delitsky pushed his way through them impatiently, ignoring the indignant voices as he elbowed his way forward. Officer Sillitoe looked round in irritation at the commotion, his expression changing to one of surprise as he realised who was causing it.

'Chief Delitsky?'

'What the hell are all these people doing here? Get them back. Right back. I want at least two vacuum doors between them and any possible hull breach.'

Spotting Sergeant Harrison, Delitsky ignored Sillitoe's mumbled excuses and hurried down the corridor to join her.

'Where's Palmer?'

Harrison indicated the med-bay. 'In there.'

'Why haven't they evacuated?'

'The Doctor thinks he can repair the suit.'

'Damned idiot,' cursed Delitsky. 'He's going to kill them all.' He reached out to open the med-bay door, but as he did so it burst open, Captain Palmer heaving Jo Teske bodily out into the corridor.

'It's going to blow!' yelled Palmer.

Delitsky closed his eyes and threw his arms up over his head, anticipating the explosion that must surely now come.

It never came.

'Hah!'

From inside the med-bay there was a cry of triumph from the Doctor, and the room abruptly went quiet.

Slowly opening his eyes, Delitsky stepped cautiously into the med-bay.

The Doctor was standing next to the gurney with his arms folded, a look of smug satisfaction on his face. Alongside him, Bill just looked exhausted. The man had done it. He had actually done it.

Delitsky crossed to the gurney, looking in disbelief at the mishmash of parts that the Doctor had discarded around the floor. Oxygen tanks, medical lasers, communicators. Even a calculator. Delitsky was no engineer, but even he could see that the Doctor had managed to effect a staggering complex repair in an incredibly short space of time using whatever he could find close at hand.

Delitsky nodded in admiration. 'Nicely done, Doctor. That's another one we owe you.'

He turned to Teske who had followed him back into the room and was now was peering in consternation at her monitor screens, trying to make sense of the readings.

'Is Baines still with us after all that?'

'Chief there's something wrong here.' She shook her head. 'These life signs are way out, and the pressure readings I'm getting just don't make sense.'

'Don't make sense how?'

'The pressure levels in the suit are precisely the opposite of what they should be,' stated the Doctor matter-of-factly. 'Instead of keeping the atmosphere of Saturn out, the settings have been readjusted to maintain that enormous pressure *inside* the suit.'

'But ... that's impossible.'

'Oh, it's perfectly possible.' The Doctor leaned close, whispering conspiratorially. 'The pressure readings and life signs don't make sense because it's not Baines inside that armour.'

Chapter

10

Cradling a cup of hot chocolate in her hand, Bill noted with dismay that a corporate canteen looked identical to the one that she worked in, even this far into the future. Stainless-steel serving counters, harsh fluorescent lighting, wipe-clean tables and uncomfortable plastic chairs. She was willing to bet that in the kitchen behind those counters they even had a deep-fat fryer for cooking chips. It was all terribly disappointing. They were in the fifty-first century, for Pete's sake! Where were the high-tech machines dispensing exotic space food? Where were the robot waiters?

She took a sip of her drink and grimaced. Even the hot chocolate was rubbish.

Jo Teske was in a seriously bad mood, annoyed by the fact that she had been concentrating so hard on Baines's unusual life signs that she had missed the huge anomaly in the pressure readings. Bill suspected it was annoying her so much because she too had a secret wish to gain the Doctor's approval.

What had put the Doctor's supposition beyond doubt was when he adjusted the sensor readings coming from the medical computer, and it swiftly become clear that the life signs being displayed on the screens were anything but human.

That left three very important questions. Where was Baines? What exactly was the alien inside the armour? And who had attempted to kill it?

Faced with so many unknowns, and with no desire to put any more of his crew in danger, Delitsky had had no other choice than to shut things down, standing down all crews and suspending mining operations on the rig until further notice.

As he left to explain his decision to Nettleman and Rince (a task that Bill could tell he was not looking forward to at all), he had ordered Captain Palmer to put a twenty-four-hour guard on the med-bay. No one was to go near the alien until he had explicit instructions from Kollo-Zarnista head office and the Federation First Contact Team.

Jo Teske had tried to argue that the figure lying in the med-bay was still a patient, alien or not, and she had a duty to try and help, but Delitsky had clearly had enough for the day.

'Nobody goes near it, Jo. Not you, not the Doctor. You hear me? Captain Palmer, I expect you to carry out my orders. Use your g-Tasers if you have to!'

And that had been that. He had swept from the med-bay, leaving Palmer to the task of clearing everybody out and putting guards on the door. Now Bill, Jo and the Doctor were sitting in the canteen staring despondently into their drinks.

'It's ridiculous,' Jo complained. 'We need to find out what happened to Baines. If we can communicate with … with whatever it is, then perhaps it can tell us.'

The Doctor said nothing. He had his elbows on the table, his chin resting on steepled fingers. He was obviously deep in in thought. Or … Bill frowned. Was he just asleep?

'Well, I'm not wrong, am I?' Realising that she wasn't going to get anything from the Doctor, Jo had turned to Bill, obviously needing to unburden her frustration on someone. Anyone.

Bill shrugged. What Jo was saying seemed pretty reasonable, but Delitsky's orders had been pretty clear, and he didn't strike her as a man who changed his mind easily.

'Perhaps if you could persuade Captain Palmer?'

On cue, Laura Palmer pushed open the double doors of the canteen and made her way over to the coffee machine. She looked exhausted, and Bill suddenly felt a pang of guilt at all the trouble she and the Doctor had caused her.

No. Bill corrected herself. All the trouble that *the Doctor* had caused her. She was just being dragged along in his wake. As usual.

Pulling up a chair beside them, Palmer slumped down into it.

'Laura, you've got to let me examine whatever is in that suit.' Jo Teske leaned forward urgently. She was obviously not going to give up easily.

'You heard the Chief's orders,' said Palmer wearily.

'But Baines—'

'Look,' snapped Palmer irritably. 'Do you imagine that anyone is more concerned about Baines than Delitsky?' Her voice softened. 'Jo, we're all strung out, and I'm really not in the mood for a fight. I'm sure that as soon as Delitsky has got in touch with head office, then you'll be able to examine … whatever it is in there. But until then, I can't let you in there.'

'What if you could talk to it without going in there?' The Doctor had opened one eye and was watching the two women with interest.

'What?'

'I've got plenty of equipment in the TARDIS that could probably do it …' Bill could see a mischievous glint in the Doctor's eye.

'Oh, no …' Captain Palmer was clearly not happy about this plan to circumnavigate her orders.

Jo Teske obviously had no such qualms. 'The Chief's orders were not to let anyone into the med-bay. He didn't say anything about us finding a way to communicate.'

'No.'

126

'Where did the TARDIS end up, by the way?' asked the Doctor innocently. 'The crew in the hangar mentioned something about moving it to the equipment bay.'

'Doctor, please.' Laura Palmer was starting to get frustrated now. 'I'm stretched enough as it is, I really don't want to have to put a guard detail on your ship as well.'

The Doctor raised an eyebrow. 'I really hope that you are not intending to deny me access to my ship, after all the help I've been giving you.'

Bill glared at him. He really could be such a jerk sometimes. Needling people just so that he could study their reactions. She took another sip of hot chocolate. It really was disgusting. She pushed the paper cup to one side. There had to be something better than this. Pushing her chair back from the table, she meandered back to the drinks dispenser, casting her eyes over the various beverages that it offered. Perhaps the coffee would be better.

As she reached out for the button, the lighting in the canteen changed abruptly, changing from harsh white to a deep red. For a moment Bill wondered if this was some new emergency, some new danger, but no one else in the canteen was paying the slightest notice to the change of mood.

Mentally kicking herself, Bill realised that the rig operated a system of artificial night, adjusting the lighting to give the crew a clearly defined 'day' and 'night'. As if to confirm her theory, the few crewmembers still present in the canteen began to make their way out, yawning and muttering their goodnights to colleagues.

With the lighting change came a noticeable drop in temperature. Suddenly feeling distinctly chilly, Bill looked around for her jacket, and then remembered with dismay that she had left it in the med-bay. She glanced over at the Doctor, but he, Jo and Captain Palmer were so engrossed in their argument that they were barely even aware of her.

Figuring that she wouldn't bother disturbing them, Bill hurried across the canteen and out into the corridor.

For the second time that day, the delicate sensors of COM-RADE 561 detected an unauthorised transmission from Kollo-Zarnista Mining Facility 27 and, once again, its attempts to fulfil its function and alert the security mainframe to that fact were blocked by a series of complicated commands that immediately set up a programming conflict inside its positronic net.

As circuit diagnostics attempted to resolve the dilemma, the transmission data flowed unimpeded through its subspace relay.

'Raptor, this is Ringbearer, are you there?'

'Of course I'm still here. Where else did you think I'd be? What's going on up there? Have you got any more information about those two strangers yet?'

'No, no they don't show up on any Federation file.'

'So, they're not undercover Feds, then. At least that's good news.'

'Forget about those two for a minute. There's something else going on here. There's been another accident.'

'Another one? Safety standards must really be slipping.'

'No, listen … They're saying that it was sabotage.'

'Sabotage? Then surely your two strangers …'

'It's not them. The man stopped it becoming a disaster.'

'Look, I'm not liking the sound of all this. If we have to pull out …'

'No, no. Please, you can't.'

'Then find out what's going on and get things back on schedule. Raptor out.'

As she made her way towards the med-bay, Bill noted that the dim red lighting of the artificial night gave the entire mine a completely different feel. It reminded her of a submarine movie that she had watched on Netflix round at Shireen's flat a few days ago …

She stopped for a moment, unable to stop herself grinning. It really was only a few weeks ago that her life had been completely normal, and yet, here she was, in the future, on a space station orbiting Saturn. Somehow watching a movie on Netflix was never going to be able to top that.

Rubbing her arms to keep warm, she set off along the corridor towards the med-bay. Unlike earlier the entire rig seemed virtually deserted now. Presumably now that operations had ceased and 'night' had fallen the crew were all in their cabins watching whatever the fifty-first-century equivalent of Netflix might be. Or in the bar.

Just as with her observations in the canteen, Bill was surprised how ordinarily *human* everything was. She might be thousands of years into her planet's future, but life still seemed to revolve around the same old routines of eating, sleeping and working. Weirdly, it made her feel optimistic … The human race had launched itself into space bringing all that was good and bad about the species with them. There were still people who seemed open, and honest, and friendly, others who were mean, stupid and greedy.

The door to the med-bay came into view around the gentle curve of the corridor and Bill saw that, ironically, one of those mean, stupid people was sitting right in front of her. The guard that Palmer had placed on duty was Officer Sillitoe.

Apparently startled by her approach, he jerked out of his chair, glaring at her suspiciously. 'What are you doing here?' he growled. 'Delitsky said you weren't allowed in here.'

'Actually, he said that the Doctor and Jo weren't allowed in here,' said Bill firmly.

Sillitoe frowned, obviously struggling to remember exactly what his orders were. The Doctor had been right. He really wasn't the sharpest knife in the drawer.

'What do you want?'

'My jacket.' Bill nodded towards the door. 'I left it on the chair next to the bed.'

'Well, you can't have it. No one is allowed in there.'

'I'm cold!'

'Tough luck.'

'But it's right there!' Bill pointed through the glass door. Her denim jacket was clearly visible draped over the back of the plastic chair next to the gurney. 'Look, if you aren't allowed to let me into the room then fine, but there's nothing stopping you going in there and getting it for me, is there?' She folded her arms and raised an eyebrow at him questioningly. 'Or are you so junior you have to get permission from Captain Palmer or Sergeant Harrison to do that?'

That did the trick.

'All right, all right. Jeez …' Sillitoe rolled his eyes and tapped in the entry code that opened the door.

Bill had to stifle a laugh. 'Easy,' she murmured.

'What?'

'I said "Thanks".' She smiled sweetly at him.

Grumbling under his breath, Sillitoe crossed the room to the bedside and snatched up the jacket from the chair. As he turned back towards the door, Baines, or rather the thing inhabiting Baines's suit, suddenly sat up.

Before Bill could utter a word of warning, a metal arm lashed out, swiping Sillitoe off his feet. Bill watched in horror as the security guard's body arced across the room, crashing into a medicine cabinet and landing in a shower of metal trays and broken glass. Bill hurried forward to help him, but the armoured suit heaved itself off the gurney, wires and cables tearing from the wall as it lurched towards her, getting between her and the motionless Sillitoe.

'Sillitoe! Wake up!' yelled Bill. 'Officer Sillitoe, you've got to wake up!'

The suit stopped, the huge metal helmet inclining slightly as if listening. Then it turned its attention to the prone security officer lying in front of it and raised a huge foot.

'No!' yelled Bill in horror. She dashed forward, snatching up a bottle from the floor and hurling it with all her might.

She ducked as the creature swung at her viciously, smashing the bottle out of the air, the huge arm missing the top of her head by inches. Lunging forwards, Bill grabbed Sillitoe by the shoulders, heaving with all her strength desperately trying to pull him backwards. As she did so, she lost her footing amongst the scattered contents of the medical cabinet and crashed to the floor.

The suit lumbered forward like some huge metallic Frankenstein's monster, the armoured boots slamming down onto the floor like sledgehammers with every step. Looming over them it raised two huge fists. Bill threw up an arm to ward off the blow, already knowing how futile a gesture it was.

From the far side of the room came two deep 'thuds' that rattled the teeth in Bill's head. The armoured suit staggered backwards, arms flailing as it struggled to stay upright.

In the doorway, Bill could see Palmer and Harrison, their gravity-Tasers trained on the metallic monster. Covered by Harrison, Captain Palmer moved swiftly across the room. She fired again and this time the gravity pulse sent the armour toppling backwards. It landed hard back on the gurney, which collapsed with a deafening crash.

Bill felt a hand grip her own, and looked up into the face of the Doctor. He hauled her to her feet.

'You OK?'

Bill nodded. 'Thanks.'

'How's he?' The Doctor looked down at Jo Teske who was trying to bring Sillitoe around.

'He's out cold. Possible fractured ribs, and there could be a concussion.'

'You can save the detailed diagnosis for later,' Palmer barked at them. 'Just get him out of here!'

The Doctor might have been unused to being shouted at, but he also knew when it was counterproductive to argue. With an ease that took Bill by surprise, he heaved Sillitoe's unconscious body off the floor, hoisting him onto his shoulders in a fireman's lift.

'Ladies first.'

They hurried out of the medical bay, the Doctor taking care with each step not to trip on the scattered contents of the cabinet. Satisfied that they were out of harm's way, Palmer followed, the gun in her hand never wavering from the armoured figure as it struggled to regain its feet. As soon as they were all safely out in the corridor she stabbed at the keypad, locking the door behind them.

The Doctor gave a snort of derision. 'Fat lot of good that's going to do. Glass.' He rapped a knuckle on the door, just to emphasise his point.

Bill rolled her eyes. 'You've got a better idea, of course.'

'Of course I do, I'm the Doctor. But I do rather have my hands full at the moment.' The Doctor indicated the unconscious security officer slung over his shoulder. 'Where can we take him?'

'My quarters,' said Teske. 'I should have enough bits and pieces there to make him comfortable.'

Miners and support staff had started to emerge from their cabins now, curious as to what the commotion in the corridor was. Jo waved a couple of them over, and between them they gently lifted Sillitoe from the Doctor's shoulders.

They slowly began to make their way down the corridor when the door to the med-bay exploded outwards in a shower of fragmented glass.

The Doctor grabbed Bill by the hand and dragged her to one side as the suited creature emerged into the corridor.

'Harrison,' yelled Palmer. 'Help me take him down.'

'No, wait!' The Doctor waved frantically at her to stop, but it was too late. Bill huddled into the Doctor's side as the two officers opened fire with their g-Tasers. Gravity pulses whipped past them, and there was a flicker of energy as they were deflected from the armoured suit, shattering what was left of the door into fragments. Glass crunching underfoot, the creature turned and started to advance along the corridor. There were screams of panic as the crewmembers in its path fled.

'You can't stop him with those,' bellowed the Doctor. 'Look.'

He pointed at two bulges on the shoulders of the suit. Bill could see they were now glowing with a strange green light.

Palmer groaned. 'He's engaged the gravity inverters.'

'Exactly. All the time he's been in the medical bay the suit has been recharging. Now, given that it was designed to withstand the gravitational pull of Saturn, using gravity pulse weapons is at bit like shooting at it with a peashooter, yes?'

Palmer swore loudly. 'All right, Harrison, we're going to have to come up with another plan.'

'How about this one?'

All eyes turned to the Doctor.

'Wait.'

'Wait?' Palmer glared at him. 'Wait for what?'

'That suit has no armaments, correct?'

'Not as such, no, but whatever is inside that armour, it could still make a mess of this place if it wanted.'

'But it's given no indication of that being the intention.'

'It just tried to kill a man!'

'The creature woke up from a major trauma after someone interfered with the controls on its pressure system. It's probably frightened and in shock.' The Doctor pointed towards the suit as it lumbered along the corridor. 'So, the question is, where do we think that the big fella is going now?'

'The canteen?' offered Bill. 'Perhaps it's hungry.'

The Doctor shot her a disparaging look.

'The service lift,' said Palmer.

'Exactly.'

'It's heading back down to the hangar.'

Bill was puzzled. 'But why is it going back there?'

The Doctor's eyes were sparkling. 'Because it's going to get its friends.'

Chapter

11

Jorgen Delitsky sat in the cool, quiet calm of the control centre, glad for a few moments just to sit and think. Even though he spent virtually every moment of his working day here, there was something about the place when it was empty that he found relaxing. The red 'night' lighting, the background hum of the machinery, the pattern of the lights blinking on the consoles, even the slight breeze from the air-con all combined to create something that he found almost tranquil.

He was well aware that Jo Teske thought that he was crazy. Most of his team couldn't wait to get away at the end of the shift, hurrying to meet friends or lovers in the bar or the cinema or the rec room. Delitsky had never been able to relax anywhere like that. He was always aware of people being slightly tense around him, of modifying their behaviour because 'the boss' was present. That in turn made him uncomfortable and so he tended to retreat here instead.

'Penny for them, Chief?'

He became aware that Claire Robbins was watching him curiously. There was always one senior officer on duty in the control room in case of emergencies, and Robbins had drawn the short straw this evening.

'I was just wondering which of the rim planets might need a man with my talents … What do you think, Claire, can you see me cutting down trees on Androzani Major?'

'Hm … Dunno, Chief. I've never seen you as the outdoor type.' She gave him a sympathetic smile. 'Things really looking that bad?'

Delitsky sighed. He had just used emergency powers to overrule two senior Kollo-Zarnista executives and bring a multi-billion-dollar mining facility to a complete standstill, he had evidence of diamond theft and sabotage taking place amongst his crew, he had lost a miner overboard and now there was a previously unknown alien species lying in his medical bay.

'Yeah … I really think that they might be.'

He suddenly felt annoyed with himself for being so downbeat. He was damned if he was just going to give in to the likes of Nettleman and Rince. This was his rig and every decision he had made had been for the right reasons. The problem was, no one back on Earth had the slightest inkling of what was going on yet.

He pulled himself out of the command chair and stretched. 'What's the status with long-range communications? Is that storm still screwing things up?'

Robbins glanced down at her control console and shrugged. 'It's still blowing force ten, but it's moving. Another hour, I guess, and we should be able to punch through the static. Until then, it's short-range comms only.'

Delitsky nodded. 'Let me know as soon as things improve. Oh, and Claire? Make sure my report goes before Nettleman's, OK.'

She grinned. 'Got it, Chief.'

Draining the last dregs of cold coffee from his mug, Delitsky was about to make his way to the machine in the corner for a refill when movement from inside the hangar caught his eye. As he watched the doors to the service elevator slid open, and a suit of pressure armour emerged.

The coffee cup slipped from Delitsky's fingers as he watched the armoured figure stamp across the hangar towards the mining bell. There was a sharp intake of breath from behind him. Robbins had spotted it too.

Seemingly oblivious to them, the armoured figure crossed the hangar to where the other suits of pressure armour stood in neatly ordered ranks, abandoned in the middle of preparation for use as soon as Delitsky had called a halt to mining operations. It stood there for a moment, almost like an officer inspecting troops on parade, then turned and strode towards a portable control console standing in the corner of the hangar. As they watched, it reached out with massive steel hands, operating the controls with surprising dexterity.

'What is it doing?' whispered Robbins staring at the massive figure hunched over the console.

Delitsky suddenly realised exactly what it intended to do and scrambled to get back into his control chair. 'Claire! Sound the general alarm!'

'Sir!'

'And tell Palmer to get a security team down here!'

The tranquil calm that Delitsky had been enjoying was abruptly shattered as, for the second time that day, emergency alarms blared around the control room.

Delitsky scrabbled frantically at the keyboard on the panel in front of him, desperately trying to dredge up seldom-used security codes and passwords from his memory. All the lights on control panel to his left suddenly went off, and console shut down with a soft click.

'No, no, no.'

Robbins had realised what it was attempting too. 'Chief, it's using the override protocols.'

'I know, I know.' Sweat beading on his forehead, Delitsky punched code after code into the computer, but as more and more panels went dead around him he realised with cold dread that he wasn't going to succeed. However fast he worked, the creature in the hangar was working faster.

He punched the console in frustration as the final panel on his console shut down. As if to taunt him, the words 'OVERRIDE PROTOCOLS ENGAGED' started to scroll across the screen above his head.

'How did it know?' he snarled in frustration.

'Because all the time it's been lying in the medical bay it's been hardwired into your mainframe.'

Delitsky turned to see the Doctor standing there. Behind him more and more people were beginning to hurry into the room. Palmer and Harrison had their g-Tasers out. It didn't take a genius to work out what had happened. His heart sank as Nettleman and Rince appeared in the doorway. No doubt they'd both have something to say about this.

The Doctor strode across to the observation window. 'You didn't bother locking him out of your systems because you thought that it was Baines in the armour, but at the same time as it's been recharging, our visitor has also been learning, studying, absorbing data.'

He peered down at what was unfolding in the hangar below with interest.

'Baines was a senior mining technician, yes? Presumably with a fairly high level of security clearance. Well, now it probably knows as much about this rig's computer systems as Baines did.'

Delitsky hauled himself from his now useless command position and turned on Palmer angrily. 'I told you to keep a guard on that thing. How the hell did it get past you?'

'Yes, Captain,' snapped Nettleman. 'I think we'd all like an answer.'

Palmer ignored him, holding Delitsky's gaze. 'There was nothing we could do, Chief. As long as it's got its gravity inverters active we've no way of stopping it without risking damage to the hull.'

'So you just let it walk down here and take control of my rig?'

'The Doctor thought that—'

'I don't give a damn what the Doctor thinks, Captain Palmer. It's you that I pay to keep this rig secure, not him. Now what do you suggest we do about this?'

Delitsky stabbed a finger at the suited figure in the hangar below. Having ensured that it wouldn't be interrupted, it had now grasped hold of one of the empty suits of mining armour and was dragging it into the open mining bell.

As the crew watched helplessly from the control room, it remerged from the bell to grab hold of another suit of armour, then another, and another.

'How many of those things were down there?' asked Rince nervously.

'Five,' murmured the Doctor quietly.

'What?' Delitsky snapped.

'There are five of them,' repeated the Doctor. 'Look.'

Having loaded four of the armoured suits into the Bell, the creature in Baines's suit had turned its attention back to the controls.

'Having worked out that they can survive in our low pressure environment inside the pressure armour, it's going back down to bring up the other four.'

'He's activating the automatic drop procedures, Chief,' Robbins called from her console. 'The only way you're going to stop him now is …' She paused. '… Is if you Purge.'

'Purge?' The Doctor looked at Delitsky accusingly.

Delitsky glared at Robbins, then gave a sigh of resignation. 'It's a last-ditch emergency device. It severs the winch cables and releases main hangar doors, jettisoning the bell.'

'Letting it fall to the centre of Saturn.'

'I've got to think about the safety of my crew, Doctor.' He strode across to his console. 'It's doubtful that that "thing" can know about it. It's not something widely known outside senior operational personnel. Hardly surprising. Would you go down in that bell if you knew there people in charge who had the option of cutting you adrift?' From the tone of his voice, the Purge was an operation that Delitsky didn't approve of. 'Since it doesn't know about it, it's unlikely that it's been able to lock out those circuits.'

'Delitsky …' The Doctor placed a hand on the Rig Chief's shoulder. 'Don't.'

Delitsky turned to yell at the Doctor, but there was something about the man's expression that made him stop.

'We know so little about these creatures. They could be a previously unknown species, a whole new life form living in the clouds of Saturn, hidden for thousands, for millions of years. They could simply be visitors. They could be stranded here. They could be so many things, I really just don't know.'

He looked pointedly at the controls that Delitsky was about to activate.

'What I do know is that if you use that, then we lose any chance that we have of ever finding out what they are or why they are here. Yes, I know we haven't exactly had the perfect house guest, but it's been alone, in a totally hostile environment, and someone on this rig has already made an attempt to kill it. I think it deserves the opportunity to rescue its friends, and explain its actions, don't you?'

Delitsky was silent for a moment, then gave a deep sigh, and nodded. 'All right, Doctor. Let's give it the benefit of the doubt.'

The Doctor smiled, and the two men turned and watched as the huge hangar doors snapped open, and mining bell started its long decent into the atmosphere of Saturn.

The control room had become uncannily quiet as everyone just stood and waited. It had now been over ten minutes since the bell had dropped into the atmosphere of the planet below.

'Any sign of movement yet?' asked Delitsky impatiently

'No.' Claire Robbins shook her head. 'They're still stationary at the same coordinates where we lost contact with Baines.'

Delitsky glanced at Teske. 'Life readings?'

The medic was staring at her screens in amazement. 'It's incredible. I've never seen readings anything like this before.'

'Captain Palmer.' Delitsky turned to his security officer. 'Recommendations, please?'

'We've no idea what we're facing here, Chief. It might be wise to get some backup.'

'Backup?'

'My security team on this rig is just six, Chief …' She let that fact just hang there.

Delitsky nodded. 'Claire, any joy with those long-range comms yet?'

'Not yet, Chief.'

'I need to know that they are back up the moment you do.'

The Doctor had been listening to their exchange with a concerned look. Bill nudged him. 'What do you think they are?' she whispered.

'I don't know,' said the Doctor. 'A high-pressure life form of some kind.'

'So, they're … Saturanians or something? They live on Saturn?'

'That's what we are about to find out.' The Doctor tapped a finger on the screen. 'Bell ascending.'

As the huge winches started to reel the bell back towards the rig, the Doctor could see the security team tensing, fingers tightening on the triggers of their weapons. The actions taken by the people in this room during the next few minutes were crucial. First contact with a new species could go one of two ways, and he knew from bitter experience what the consequences could be if things went badly.

He glanced across at Captain Palmer, but the young security captain was looking cool and collected, hands well away from the weapon on her belt. The Doctor allowed himself a moment of optimism. There were good people in this room. Palmer, Teske, Delitsky …

His gaze shifted to the frightened faces of Nettleman and Rince. Then again, there were always wild cards …

The massive winches suddenly started to slow.

'Here we go,' murmured Bill nervously.

It seemed as though everyone in the control room was holding their breath. Then, in a cloud of methane vapour, the mining bell emerged through the hatch, like a magician appearing through a stage trapdoor in a puff of smoke. With a blare on the klaxons the hangar doors swung shut with a clang that shook the floor, then total silence descended on the control room.

Every pair of eyes in the control room was now focused on the sphere sitting on the floor of the hangar. Delitsky was half in, half out of his chair, watching the hatch with bated breath.

There was a sudden hiss of hydraulics, and the Doctor felt Bill jump alongside him as the hatch started to open. One by one, five huge armoured figures pulled themselves from the pod, making their way clumsily down the walkway and lining up in front of the control room window.

For a moment they just stopped, silent and motionless, then one of them stepped forward, raising an armoured hand as if in greeting. A distorted cracking voice hissed from the speakers.

'We are the Ba-El Cratt. We wish to claim asylum on this station.'

Chapter

12

Laura Palmer had to admit that her account of *this* tour of duty was definitely going to raise a few eyebrows when she finally got around to writing her memoirs. Assuming that everything wasn't completely hushed up by the intelligence services, of course. During her time at the Academy she had heard plenty of rumours of clandestine agencies within the Federation that dealt with situations like this, and had no wish to find out whether those rumours were true or not. She was just glad that Delitsky was taking charge of things rather than Nettleman.

As always she had nothing but total respect for the Rig Chief. Despite having already had to put up with a day that would have reduced a lesser man to a gibbering wreck, he was dealing with this latest development with a coolness that she wished she felt herself.

By contrast, Nettleman and Rince (two perfect examples of 'lesser men') were cowering near the door to the control room, looking just about ready to run screaming.

Watching everything was the Doctor, his expression indecipherable. Laura had never met anyone so difficult to read. There were times when he seemed to treat everything going on around him as if it was just some kind of elaborate game, and yet, when it had mattered, he had been quick to act in a way that had already saved countless lives. She just wished that she knew his ultimate intentions.

Her pulse rate started to increase as Delitsky took a step towards the hangar windows, confronting the aliens below. As he did so, Laura noticed, he positioned himself close enough to his control console that he could reach the Purge control for the hangar. As she watched, his fingers started to slowly tap in the release codes that would allow him to open the doors and vent the entire hangar into space. The Doctor obviously noticed it too, and she saw his lips tightening in concern.

'I'm Jorgen Delitsky.' The Rig Chief's voice boomed through the speakers. 'I'm in charge here. You say I'm addressing the Ba-El Cratt – well, what are you and where do you come from?'

One of the five armoured figures stepped forwards, the featureless helmet tilting backwards as if staring up through the glass observation window.

'We come from a system many light years from here,' came the sibilant, whispering voice. 'We are refugees from our home world, fleeing an aggressor that has virtually wiped us out. Extensive damage to our engines caused our ship to crash into the planet below. We have been trapped for many planetary cycles.'

'You say you want asylum here, and yet you've attacked us.'

'We apologise for any distress we have caused. We have tried numerous methods of making contact, but our species are very different to each other. In the end, direct action, and the use of your pressure vessels, was the only course left open to us.'

'Killing one of my crew in the process.'

Laura could tell that Delitsky was struggling to keep the anger from his voice.

'Your crewman is not dead.'

Excited muttering filled the control room at that revelation. Delitsky shushed them angrily.

'Baines is still alive?'

'He is safe on board our ship.'

Laura watched as the Doctor's brow furrowed, and a look of confusion settled across his features. It was obvious that he didn't believe that.

Delitsky was obviously having a hard time believing it too. 'Our sensors have picked up no evidence of any ship.'

'It is deep within the atmosphere of the planet,' explained the hissing voice. 'Far deeper than your primitive sensors are able to penetrate. If you will allow us asylum here, we can work with you to recover our ship. And your crewman.'

Turning off the comms channel, Delitsky turned to face his crew.

'Well, thoughts?'

Jo Teske stepped forwards. 'If there's any chance that Baines is still alive …'

'Yeah, I know.' He looked across at Laura. 'Captain Palmer?'

Laura thought for a moment, wanting to choose her words carefully. 'The Ba-El Cratt are talking of asylum, of wanting refuge from an aggressor. That means there's something hostile out there, and if it starts to look as though we're taking sides …' She paused. 'Chief, if there is any possibility that this is going to turn into a war, we are simply not equipped to deal with it. If there's a chance of saving Baines then I agree with Dr Teske that we should take steps to recover him, but I think we need that backup. I think that we should request a gunship from the barracks on Ganymede immediately.' She shot a look at the Doctor, suddenly feeling a need to reassure him of her intentions. 'Just as a precaution.'

Laura could see Nettleman pushing his way across the room, voicing his protest at Delitsky's decision.

'This is a Kollo-Zarnista matter, Delitsky. You cannot allow the military to take any kind of action in this facility without direct orders from the board.'

'This has gone way beyond the jurisdiction of Kollo-Zarnista,' snarled Delitsky angrily. 'There are five aliens in the hangar, Nettleman. Five members of a previously uncontacted species. That makes it a Federation matter!'

'But do you really think that it's necessary to involve the military?' The Doctor also didn't seem happy about it.

'Yes, I do,' said Delitsky, obviously satisfied that his senior team were all on the same page as him. 'Robbins. I don't care what the systems tell you about storm interference, I want a priority channel to Colonel Vanezis on Ganymede, right now.'

'Yes. Sir.' Claire Robbins hurried to her console.

'What do you want to do about these five, Chief?' asked Palmer indicating the aliens in the hangar.

Delitsky was just drawing breath to answer when the back blew off the communications console.

The Doctor ducked as sparks and flames spat across the control room. Total panic descended as people dived for cover, fearful of another explosion. He quickly snatched a fire extinguisher from the wall and hurried towards the burning console. As the clouds of billowing gas smothered the flames, Robbins staggered to her feet, coughing and spluttering. Casting the extinguisher aside, the Doctor helped her to a chair.

Jo Teske was there in an instant, checking her hands and face for burns.

'I'm OK,' coughed Robbins.

'You were lucky,' said Jo grimly.

The Doctor agreed. The force of the blast had been directed away from her. It hadn't been a big explosion, but if she'd been in the path of it … He crouched down and peered into the smoking remains of the comms console.

Bill scurried nervously to his side, nose wrinkling at the smell of scorched plastic that now filled the control room. 'What happened?'

'She was cut off,' said the Doctor, grimly inspecting the shattered circuits. 'By someone who really didn't want that message to get out.'

Bill's eyes widened. 'A bomb?'

'No, not exactly.' The Doctor peered into the charred mess. 'My guess is that someone rewired things so that when the transmitter was brought up to full power it would overload.'

'You mean more sabotage.' Delitsky was standing behind them, staring in the wrecked console in disbelief.

'I would say so, wouldn't you?' The Doctor's face was grim.

'But who?' Delitsky jerked a thumb at the hangar window. 'Them?'

'How?' The Doctor raised a quizzical eyebrow. 'There's only been one of the Ba-El Cratt here until now, and never left alone. Besides, the first sabotage attempt was directed against them.' He stood up, wiping the ash and soot from his hands. 'No, your saboteur is someone a little closer to home, which brings us to the question of what are you going to do with your guests?' The Doctor looked pointedly at the Purge control on Delitsky's control console. 'After all, the hangar bay might not be the safest place for them to stay …'

Realising what he was intimating, Delitsky crossed to his desk and disarmed the Purge control. 'All right, Doctor? What do you suggest?'

The Doctor pursed his lips, pondering the various options. A sudden thought struck him. 'The medical bay has a decompression chamber, doesn't it?'

'Yes.'

'Well, then. If it's capable of recreating the pressures below us then it would seem to offer our guests an alternative environment to the pressure armour. Let them slip into something more comfortable, so to speak.'

'That makes sense, Jorgen.' Jo Teske had been listening to their conversation. 'If we can persuade even one or two of them to use the pressure chamber then it gives us a chance to recycle the batteries in the suits. We're not really equipped to keep five suits of armour powered up simultaneously. It gives us a bit of breathing space to come up with some better solutions, plus …' She paused. 'It's secure, easy to put a guard on it, if you still have any worries about them.'

'Oh, I've plenty of worries. About them, about Baines, about the saboteur on this rig …' He thought for a moment, then made a decision. 'OK, Jo. Get onto it.'

'I'll need Jenloz to help.'

Delitsky shook his head. 'I need him to repair this.' He pointed at the wrecked communication console.

'I can do that,' said the Doctor.

Delitsky regarded him carefully. 'Another hidden talent, Doctor?'

'Oh yes.' The Doctor nodded. 'Mine rescue, pressure-suit maintenance, comms systems repairs ... Plus I'm also a dab hand with a needle and thread and can whip up a great Spaghetti Bolognese.'

'I don't doubt it.'

'Jenloz is going to be far more use to Dr Teske than I can be, and he can't be in two places at once.'

'All right, Doctor, let's see what you can do. But I want that communications system up and running within the hour.'

'Yes, Chief!' The Doctor saluted.

Scowling, Delitsky turned and strode back across the control room, barking orders as he went. 'Palmer, Harrison. I want you to escort the Ba-El Cratt from the hangar. I'm making their safety your responsibility.'

'Got yourself a job, then?'

The Doctor turned to see Bill regarding him with an amused smile on her face.

'Yes. And guess who's going to be my assistant?'

Delitsky watched as Palmer and her officers escorted the five Ba-El Cratt in their armoured suits across the hangar and into the service lift. He had told Palmer to use the gym as a holding area until they had made the necessary modifications to the pressure chamber. It wasn't ideal, but at least the gym was on the same deck as the med-bay if any problems arose.

He rubbed his hands across his face. God, they really were not equipped to deal with a situation like this. His people were miners and technicians. This situation needed skilled negotiators, experts. The military couldn't get here fast enough as far as he was concerned. Still, if the Ba-El Cratt were to be believed then Baines was still alive, although Delitsky still had no idea of how that could be possible.

'Chief Delitsky.'

Delitsky lowered his hands to see Nettleman standing in front of him. The smile on the man's face was not a pleasant one.

'What is it, Nettleman?' Delitsky had no more energy to even bother at the pretence of being polite. 'You may not have noticed, but I've got rather a lot on my plate at the moment.'

'Oh, I've noticed. I've noticed quite a lot of things.'

From the tone of Nettleman's voice Delitsky knew that he wasn't going to like what the company official was about to say.

'Earlier you very helpfully pointed out to me that in an emergency situation the regulations clearly state that all decisions and responsibility for the rig and its crew devolved to the Rig Chief.'

'That's right.' Delitsky's heart sank as he realised that this was the moment when his earlier blunt dismissal of the man was going to come back and bite him.

'Well, let me return the favour. Rince has reminded me of another regulation that states just as clearly that where any employee of Kollo-Zarnista Mining encounters evidence of, or has direct contact with, persons or objects of unknown origin that might have direct consequences for the long-term future of the company, then *all* matters relating to those persons or objects become the responsibility of the senior company official present at the time.'

Nettleman leaned uncomfortably close.

'That's me, Delitsky,' he hissed. 'So from this moment on you will take *no* decision relating to the Ba-El Cratt without checking with me first. Do I make myself clear?'

'Yes, sir.'

'No one gets access to them except me. Make sure your security grunts are aware of that.'

Without waiting for any acknowledgment, Nettleman turned and strode from the control room. As Delitsky watched him go, he became aware that his decision to put the man in his place earlier might just have had serious implications for everyone working on the rig.

* * *

'Military? What do you mean, military?'

'It's fine. Trust me.'

'Trust you? You said we'd have to deal with local security forces, not Federation gunships.'

'And you won't have to. I disabled the long-range comms before they could send the message.'

'You disabled the … You stupid idiot. That wasn't part of the plan!'

'I had no choice! I told you, we've had problems here.'

'Well, now you've got another problem, haven't you? How exactly are you going to call in the freighter if the long-range comms are disabled?'

'I … I'll think of something.'

'Oh, you'll think of something.'

'I will!'

'You better had. Or I might just come up with a plan of my own. One that you're not going to like very much. Raptor out.'

Bill watched as the Doctor buried his head in the back of the communications console, reattaching broken connectors with his sonic screwdriver, replacing shattered circuit boards. Every now and then he would lean back to hand Bill some charred and broken piece of electronics, or ask her to pass him some complex-looking tool. She was more of a general dogsbody than an assistant. She was surprised that he hadn't asked her to mop his brow or fetch him some tea.

'Are you nearly finished?'

'I'm nearly finished, *here*,' came the muffled voice, 'but I've still got to find whatever it was that caused this.'

Bill was puzzled. 'Eh?'

The Doctor pulled his head out of the console. Bill had to stop herself from laughing, his hair was sticking up wildly and there were black smudges on his nose and chin.

'Think about it,' said the Doctor, using his sonic screwdriver to reattach the back of the console. 'There's a duty officer in here twenty-four hours a day, so there's no way that anyone could get in there to do this without being noticed.'

'Unless it's the duty officer who did it,' Bill pointed out smugly.

'Robbins has been the duty officer since the accident with Baines.'

'Oh.' Given that it was Robbins who'd nearly had her hands blown off, Bill had to admit that it seemed unlikely that she was the saboteur.

The Doctor clambered to his feet, brushing soot and dirt from his jacket. 'There are hundreds of miles of cables running all over this station. Pick the right point and someone could easily blow the circuits in the control room without having to go anywhere near it.'

Bill groaned. 'You're not suggesting that we check hundreds of miles …'

'Come on.'

With that the Doctor turned and vanished out through the door of the control room. Bill scrambled to her feet and hurried after him. The Doctor was already a long way down the corridor.

'Hey, slow down.' She had to jog to catch up with him. 'Where are we going?'

'Not sure yet. Let's just follow the trail and see.'

Peering at the readings that he was getting on his sonic screwdriver, the Doctor made his way along the corridor, obviously following the trail of some hidden cable buried deep in the walls. The crew of the rig gave him a wide berth. Bill could hardly blame them. Hunched over, with his wild hair and soot-smudged face, the Doctor was quite a sight. Not that he ever seemed to care what other people thought of him.

Still following the invisible trail, the Doctor turned off from the main corridor, making his way along a narrow service passageway.

He stopped abruptly, Bill almost crashing into the back of him.

'This is the spot.'

Changing the settings in the screwdriver, he started to unfasten a wall panel. With Bill's help, they pulled it free and lowered it to the floor.

'Yes,' said the Doctor, pointing into the cavity. 'There's the problem.'

Bill looked. Several cables had been bundled together, and what looked like a wrench of some kind had been crudely taped to the infrastructure so that it bridged two metal conduits. The inside of the cavity was blackened and charred. There had obviously been some kind of fire or electrical discharge.

The Doctor reached inside the wall, pulling the tape from the wrench and tugging it free.

'It's exactly as I thought: someone has rigged this so that when the comms unit was brought up to full power it short-circuited.'

'It looks very crude.'

'Crude, but effective.' The Doctor started unravelling the knotted cables.

Bill frowned; there was something not quite right here. 'Hang on a minute. In the med-bay, the damage that was done to the pressure armour, that was delicate, complicated work, right? I mean, something that had to be done by someone who really knew what they were doing. This …' She pointed at the tangled mess. 'Well, this is the sort of thing that *I* would do. No finesse, just chuck a spanner in the works and see what breaks.'

'Oh …' The Doctor stopped, suddenly coming to the same conclusion that she had.

'This wasn't done by the same person.'

'No.' The Doctor looked at her with something that was almost approaching admiration. 'There are two saboteurs on this rig.'

Chapter

13

Standing in the lift alongside the Doctor, Bill was feeling particularly pleased with herself. It wasn't often that she was able to reach a conclusion ahead of him, so the moment needed to be savoured.

Given the unsophisticated nature of the damage, the Doctor had made swift work of the repairs, and they were now on their way to the central communication server to restart the system. The tinny, authoritative voice in the lift had announced that they were not 'authorised personnel', and that the floor they had requested was 'off limits', but the Doctor had resolved that problem fairly swiftly too.

Having finally caught sight of his reflection in the shiny aluminium door of the lift, the Doctor had tried to push his tousled grey hair into some kind of order and was now using a large, grubby paisley handkerchief to rub the soot from his face.

As the lift came to a halt and the doors slid open, Bill stepped out and looked at her surroundings in surprise. Unlike the rest of the station, which to Bill's eyes seemed like a strange amalgam of oil rig and power station, this corridor was white, virtually featureless and very, very clean.

'This way.' Stuffing the handkerchief back into his jacket pocket, the Doctor headed off down the corridor before coming to a halt in front of a large, heavy-looking door.

'Another vault?' asked Bill curiously.

'Of a kind.'

Opening a panel next to the door, the Doctor activated his sonic screwdriver once more, and the door slid upwards with a soft 'whoosh' of compressed air.

The room beyond reeked of high-end, expensive technology. Bill gave a chuckle as she remembered how impressed she had been when she had been shown inside the server room at the university. Compared to this, however, it now seemed pitiful. Row upon row of racks stretched back into the darkness, lights glowing on the fronts of the servers that they contained, the air conditioning humming gently as it pumped cool air into the room. Sitting in front of the racks, almost like some kind of altar, was a desk with a single chair and three large monitor screens.

The Doctor slid into the seat, cracking his knuckles and bringing the interface to life. Bill just tucked herself against the back wall and watched as he busied himself at the controls, looking totally at ease amongst the technology. She guessed that as far as he was concerned, this was just some children's toy, an abacus compared to the machinery in the TARDIS. She wondered if he had ever been truly awestruck by anything ...

The Doctor worked in silence for several minutes then, with a sigh of satisfaction, sat back and stretched. 'There ... That should do it.'

'Fixed?'

'It'll take a little while for the systems to calibrate, but yes. Fixed.'

Bill pulled herself from the wall, starting towards the door. 'We'd better get back to the control room, then. Tell Delitsky.'

'Hmm? The Doctor leaned forward once more, the light from the monitor screens giving his face a harsh bluish tint.

'I said we should tell Delitsky that you've fixed it.'

'Delitsky is going to call in the military as soon as he knows this is fixed, and I'm not sure that's necessarily the best idea, so it might be better to wait for a bit before we tell him. Besides, I want to look for something else whilst we're here.'

'Great.' Bill slumped back against the wall, watching as the Doctor started to bring page after page of text and schematics onto the three screens, occasionally stopping to examine something, then moving on to the next set of data.

Ten minutes went past. Then another ten. Bill yawned. Whilst they had been racing around actually *doing* something, she hadn't really had a chance to notice how tired she was. But now that she had stopped ... The combination of the hum from the air conditioning and the pattern of blinking lights on the servers was starting to make her eyelids feel heavy.

'Gotcha!'

The Doctor's cry of triumph snatched her from the brink of sleep. Rubbing at her eyes Bill wandered over to him, looking over his shoulder as information flashing across the screens at a dizzying rate.

'Found something?'

'The Ba-El Cratt spacecraft.'

Bill cast her mind back to what the aliens had told them. 'I thought they said that it was too deep in the atmosphere. That it couldn't be detected by these sensors.'

'That's what they said. But if that's the case ...' The Doctor brought up an image on the centre screen. 'Then what is that?'

Bill leaned forward to scrutinise the image. It certainly 'could' be a spacecraft of some kind, but ... 'Hang on a minute. That's not in the atmosphere, that's in the rings.'

'Yes, it is, isn't it?' The Doctor's eyes had that twinkle in them that meant that he was onto something. 'So that either means that it's *not* the Ba-El Cratt spacecraft, it's something else, or it *is* their spacecraft and they're lying to us. Whichever it is, I think it needs investigation, don't you?'

'Absolutely.' Bill grinned. 'What are we waiting for?'

'Because I've found something else.'

'Get you. You're on fire!'

The Doctor frowned at her. 'When I was rebooting the communications network I needed to scan though subspace transmissions from the rig so that I could recalibrate the system correctly.'

'If you say so.'

'This is the information the computer gave me.' He brought up another page of data onto the screen.

Bill stared at it blankly. It was just code. She shrugged. 'I really don't have any idea of what it is you think I should be able to see.'

'This,' the Doctor pointed at a line, 'is a subspace transmission that registered exactly eleven minutes ago. Think about that.'

Bill thought about it. 'You were still repairing the communications system, at that point!'

'Exactly.' He began to scroll through the data on the screen. 'And once you have that unique subspace signature, then it's easy enough to see another transmission here, and here, and here …'

'The saboteur?'

'That would be a fair guess.'

'With a transmitter of their own?'

'Yes.'

'Well then, let's find out who's been using it!' said Bill excitedly. 'Tell Delitsky that we've found his saboteur.'

'*One* of his saboteurs,' the Doctor reminded her. 'Besides, whoever is doing this is using some very sophisticated equipment to cover their tracks. The mainframe can't tell what the transmission says, where it's being sent or who is sending it. It's taken a great deal of persuasion on my part, and a promise of marriage, for it to even acknowledge that the data I've found exists.'

'So basically, Computer Says No.'

'And Delitsky strikes me as a man who likes facts, not suppositions.'

'So …' Bill shrugged. 'What next?'

'We get some slightly more sophisticated equipment than this.' He patted the console affectionately. 'No offence.'

'Back to the TARDIS?'

The Doctor nodded. 'Back to the TARDIS.'

The Doctor slid open the doors of the equipment bay and strode across the darkened room towards the TARDIS. 'Wait there a minute.' He pushed open the doors and vanished inside leaving Bill standing in the gloom.

She peered curiously at the shapes looming around her. Delitsky's crew had moved the TARDIS here after the Doctor's successful rescue of Baines, or rather, his successful rescue of the creature that was now wearing Baines's suit. The room was a mix of storage room and workshop. A long bench ran along one wall, the surface littered with complex-looking tools. Vehicles of various sizes lined the other wall: forklifts and loaders of some kind, their purpose instantly recognisable even if the individual designs were unfamiliar. Dotted here and there were pieces of pressure armour, presumably in for repair.

It reminded Bill of the shed belonging to Graham, Moira's next-door neighbour. She'd had to pop round there one day to borrow a wrench when the shower had bust. Moira didn't have a single tool in the house, of course, but Bill had remembered seeing Graham unloading a toolkit from the back of his car, so figured he'd be worth asking. He'd led her down the garden to his shed, unlocking the rusty old padlock and ushering her inside with a strange sort of pride. The interior had been the same jumble of hand tools and broken or unfinished machinery. Bill remembered that there had been hundreds of copies of *Rail Enthusiast* magazine in piles on the floor, and a half-built model of a steam locomotive on his workbench.

It suddenly struck her that there was the answer to her earlier question about what would leave the Doctor awestruck. He would be awestruck by Graham's shed.

'Here, take this.'

The Doctor re-emerged from the TARDIS and thrust a small black box into her hands. It was about the size of a television remote control, with a small display screen and two large buttons on the front – one red, one green.

'What's this?'

'More sophisticated equipment.'

'You're kidding, right?' To Bill's eyes it looked like someone had gone and bought a kid's toy from a pound store and stuck a couple of Smarties on it.

'It's an extremely sensitive subspace tracking device,' said the Doctor, ignoring the disparaging look she was giving him. 'You're going to have to work fast because the subspace disturbance from the last transmission is already fading. This should have the range to track it to its source, but the longer you leave it, the less accurate it's going to be.'

Bill regarded him suspiciously. '*I'm* going to have to work fast? What are *you* going to be doing?'

'I'm going to go and find that ship.'

'Oh, no, that's not fair …' Bill frowned. 'Hang on … I thought that you couldn't use the TARDIS. Didn't you say that the gravity whatnots would upset the space-time thingummy and affect the steering?'

The Doctor looked pained. 'Oh, I can see that all the lectures of mine that you've come to have really sunk in. Gravity whatnots? Space-time thingummy?'

'Don't avoid the question!'

'Yes, I did say that I couldn't use the TARDIS. I lied! It's what I do.'

'Why?'

'To make an impression.'

'What?'

The Doctor took a deep breath. 'Look, believe it or not, getting caught in the vault stealing diamonds wasn't exactly what I had in mind when we arrived, OK? It got us off on the wrong foot so I needed to do something that would make everybody trust us.'

'Um, hello. You tried to rescue their friend from certain death.'

'Yes, I did. And imagine if I had done that in the TARDIS. I pop into a box, the box vanishes, I reappear a few moments later with their missing miner. Ta dah! Everyone is happy, but …' The Doctor grinned. 'This way there was danger, and excitement and heroism …'

'You were showing off.'

'I was making a statement.'

'You are impossible!'

'Worked, didn't it?' The Doctor looked smug. Bill could have slapped him

'Um, are you two planning on going somewhere?'

The Doctor and Bill turned to see Captain Palmer watching them suspiciously.

'Captain Palmer, the very person.'

'Doctor. You have been a huge help, but as I told you earlier, I'm afraid that I can't allow ...'

'Captain, I don't think that you believe the Ba-El Cratt when they say that they have Baines in a spacecraft too deep in the atmosphere for us to detect.'

Palmer was silent for a moment, and then shook her head. 'No. No, I don't.'

'Of course you don't, it's a story that requires no proof from them and total trust from us, because we want to believe that they still have Baines safe and well.' The Doctor's eyes were alive with energy. 'But what would you say if I told you that I had detected a spacecraft drifting in the rings. That would be worth investigation, yes?'

Palmer stared at him. 'In the rings?'

'Yes.' Without taking his eyes from hers, the Doctor reached behind his back and pushed the TARDIS doors wide open.

Palmer's eyes widened in shocked astonishment as she caught sight of the console room beyond.

'Do you fancy accompanying me on a little trip?' asked the Doctor coyly.

'I ... I don't believe it.'

The Doctor stepped to one side as Palmer peered through the doorway.

'I just don't believe it.' Gingerly she stepped inside the police box.

Bill gave the Doctor a disapproving glare. 'You love it, don't you? Doing that big reveal.'

'It's a very useful distraction.' He held up a small bunch of different coloured plastic tags.

Bill peered at them. 'What are those?'

'Electronic keys.'

'Did you just lift those off her belt?' she asked accusingly

'Yes.'

'She'll notice!'

The Doctor gave a snort. 'No, she won't. I've just given her brain far more pressing things to process.'

Bill looked at him suspiciously. 'OK. What do you need them for?'

'I don't need them. You do.' The Doctor pressed the keys into her hand.

'Bill, listen to me.' All the playfulness had suddenly vanished from the Doctor's voice. 'I have a sneaking suspicion that our friendly alien refugees are anything but friendly. I also think that someone else here knows that already. These are security master keys; they should get you through any door. Use the tracker. Once you find that transmitter, it should give you some idea as to who is operating it. Once you know, tell Delitsky to act. Otherwise I have a feeling there is going to be another accident, and this one could be fatal.'

Bill nodded, conscious of the trust that the Doctor was placing in her.

The Doctor stepped into the TARDIS, hesitating for a moment on the threshold. 'Bill … please don't take any unnecessary chances.'

With that he vanished inside.

Bill stood back as the doors closed and the familiar wheezing, groaning sound started to echo around the room as the time ship faded from view.

Bill hefted the keys in her hand. The Doctor had trusted her with an important task. She wasn't about to let him down.

Chapter

14

Nettleman sat in the empty conference room, his mind awash with intriguing possibilities. He was all too aware that, in a career that had been spent almost exclusively in meetings, the few minutes that he had just spent with the Ba-El Cratt could possibly turn out to be the most important meeting that he had ever had.

He had listened to their tiresome sob story about war and oppression and having to flee from their home planet, nodding in all the right places, his face a carefully constructed mask of concern and sympathy. He had carefully considered their plea for asylum, making sure that they knew he was on their side, but being very clear about the fact that the decision to grant that asylum wasn't something he could take alone. Nettleman knew from past experiences that gambles this big needed the involvement of other people to take the blame if things didn't go to plan.

Perhaps, he had suggested to the Ba-El Cratt, they could offer him something that he could take to his superiors that would help make the request go through more smoothly ...

That was when the conversation had become interesting.

Nettleman had come to Kollo-Zarnista Mining Facility 27 with a plan to make himself rich. Because of all the problems on board, those plans had started to unravel, but now ... Nettleman was starting to realise just how profitable this trip could actually turn out to be.

The Ba-El Cratt could survive in the crushing pressures of the gas giants. No, it was better than that, they *thrived* in that environment. He thought about all the technology that the human race needed just to be able to work here: tonnes of equipment, hundreds of people, millions of dollars' worth of investment. Not to mention the payment in diamonds that the Cancri demanded. Yes, it was true that they provided some necessary machinery, some basic support contracts, but if he could remove the need for all that ...

In his mind's eye, Nettleman could see a new way forward for Kollo-Zarnista. The Ba-El Cratt needed asylum. Well, fine, but why shouldn't they work for it? The human race would provide them with a safe haven, sanctuary within the atmosphere of the gas giants, a security team to guard them from their enemies, and in return, they extracted the diamonds.

His heart started to pound. If he could make this work then they might not have to pay anything to mine the diamonds. They could terminate their contract with the Cancri, shut down the mines, shed hundreds of staff from the payroll. It would save the company millions. Hundreds of millions. And it would all be his doing.

Nettleman sat back in his chair, closed his eyes and started to dream about how much Kollo-Zarnista might reward him for negotiating a deal like that.

Laura was still struggling to come to terms with the space around her. For a control room of this size to be inside that … that box!

She was suddenly aware of the Doctor watching her. He was standing alongside a mushroom-like device that was obviously a control console of some kind. With a sudden jolt of panic, Laura realised that she was standing in a spacecraft of unknown origin with a man she knew practically nothing about. A man who, on the basis of the evidence around her, was probably non-terrestrial in origin.

The panic on her face must have been clear.

'Are you all right?'

Laura nodded. 'Yeah.'

'It was the rings, wasn't it?'

'I beg your pardon?'

The Doctor started to busy himself at the controls. 'The thing that made you step over the threshold, to take the leap. It wasn't the mention of a mysterious alien spaceship, it wasn't because of any suspicions you might have about the Ba-El Cratt, it wasn't even because of any hope that Baines might still be alive; it was when I mentioned the rings …'

Laura laughed, suddenly at ease without really knowing why that should be. 'Was it that obvious?'

'I've come across a few ring gazers in my life.' A warm smile played around the edges of the Doctor's lips, momentarily taking all the harshness from his features and making him seem … Younger? Or older? Laura couldn't tell.

'Ring gazer, huh? Well please don't call me that in front of any of my squad, I get enough grief from them as it is.'

'My lips are sealed.'

Laura stared around the inside of the ship, taking in the construction, the strange alien symbols, the sheer impossibility of it all. 'Well, from the look of all this, I'm guessing that you've seen a few ringed planets in your time.'

'A few. But I'll let you into a secret: Saturn is one of the best there is.'

The Doctor flicked a control, and a viewscreen flickered into life. Laura crossed to the console and stared at the image on the screen. Saturn in all its glory. She'd never get tired of it.

'You really have got it bad.' The Doctor was staring at her, clearly amused.

Suddenly embarrassed Laura forced herself to focus on the reason why they were here. 'So, this spacecraft you think you've detected in the rings …'

'*Think* I've detected?' Indignation wiped the amusement from the Doctor's face. His hands started to dance across the controls, and the image of the rings jumped in magnification. A dark smudge now nestled amongst the tumbling sea of rocks and ice. He pointed at the screen.

'To produce a smudge like that, something must have been involved in a collision that kicked up a cloud of ice and dust.'

Laura shrugged. 'It could be a natural phenomenon. A Peggy.'

The Doctor nodded approvingly. 'You know your history.'

Peggy was a moonlet, detected by accident way back in the pre-space-age era by an astronomer on Earth. The rings were full of such tiny objects.

The image jumped even nearer, and Laura leaned closer to the screen. What was floating there was unlike any ship that Laura had ever encountered before.

'As a wise man once said, "It's life, Jim, but not as we know it."'

'So why would the Ba-El Cratt lie?' she asked him. 'Why tell us that their ship was lost in the atmosphere?'

'Shall we go aboard and find out?'

* * *

'Come on, you stupid thing.' Bill shook the tracker angrily. For a highly sophisticated, super-sensitive tracking device it was being extremely temperamental. It was like trying to get a 3G signal in Cabot Circus shopping centre, but at least there she knew that if you stood outside PC World, with your phone held in the air for long enough, then you'd eventually get a signal.

On impulse she did exactly that, stretching as high as she could and waving the tracker back and forth. Fortunately everyone else in the corridor was far too busy with more important matters to pay her much heed and, apart from one or two curious glances from people as they hurried past, most of the crew simply ignored her. Even so, she was glad that she had had the initiative to grab a discarded boiler suit from the equipment bay and pull it on over her own clothes. At least now she didn't stand out like a sore thumb quite so much.

When she had initially turned the tracker on, the signal had been clear and easy to follow, leading her out of the equipment bay and up into the crew quarters. That's when things had started to go wrong. As the Doctor had warned, the signal had swiftly started to fade, and Bill had found it more and more difficult to make sense of the readings that it was giving her.

She was positive that the transmitter had to be located on this deck somewhere, but there were literally hundreds of crew cabins, and even if by some miracle all of them were unoccupied, searching every single one was going to be a virtually impossible task.

To her amazement the tracker suddenly gave a beep, and the soft pinging noise that had led her this far resumed once more.

'Finally!' Bill lowered the tracker and studied the readout. If she was reading it correctly then the source of the signal was really, really close.

Praying that the machine wouldn't pack up on her again, Bill made her way along the corridor, swinging the tracker to and fro in front of her, the pings it was making getting closer and closer together, and higher and higher in pitch.

The noise reached a crescendo and Bill found herself standing outside a door with a sign reading '*Guest Quarters. Executive Personnel*'. She looked at the nameplate that had been affixed below it. '*Donald Nettleman*'.

'Gotcha.' Bill nodded with satisfaction. The man was a weasel. She'd enjoy exposing him.

As she reached in the pocket of her boiler suit for the security keys that the Doctor had given her, the noise from the tracker became even more frantic. Surprised, Bill looked down at the readings. The signal was actually coming from the room next door.

Bill stared at the sign on that door. '*Clive Rince*'. The saboteur wasn't Nettleman. It was Rince.

Quickly checking the corridor to see that there was nobody watching, Bill pulled the keys from her pocket, realising that she had never asked the Doctor how they worked. There was a small silver plate next to the door. Presumably you just placed the key on the plate? She did so, and to her relief the door slid open with a hiss. Bill hurried inside.

The room was sparse and functional, a cross between a ship's cabin and a low-budget hotel room. There was a bed, a desk, a small en-suite shower room, but everything was cold, metal and plastic. Bill swung the tracker around the room; the signal was staring to fade again, far more rapidly than before. She was running out of time.

On impulse, she hurried over to the shower room, leaning inside and waving the tracker around the interior. Nothing. There was barely enough room for the toilet and the sink, let alone anything else.

As she stepped back into the bedroom the signal suddenly peaked, then abruptly went dead. It was enough of a confirmation, though. The transmitter was in here somewhere. Quickly, she started to search, pulling open drawers and cupboards, but there didn't seem to be anything in them other than clothes and paperwork. There had to be a concealed compartment or something. Stepping inside, she started to check the walls and floor. After five minutes of searching she had still found nothing, and was on the verge of giving up when something in the ceiling caught her eye. A loop of cable had somehow become trapped between one of the ceiling panels and the stainless steel wall. She reached up to try to pull it free, but the cable was tightly wedged. Excitedly, Bill realised that the entire ceiling panel must come loose. That was where the transmitter had to be hidden.

She pulled the metal chair from under the desk into the middle of the room and clambered onto it. As she stood there on tiptoe trying to work out the release mechanism, she suddenly became aware of footsteps behind her.

Someone had entered the room.

Laura had watched in disbelief as the Doctor emerged from the bowels of his spacecraft with a couple of bright orange spacesuits bundled up in his arms.

'You've got to be kidding. We can't go out there in those!'

'Why not?' The Doctor had dumped the suits on the floor of the console room and, discarding his jacket, started to struggle into one of them.

'It's Saturn. We'll need gravity inverters.'

'We've got them.' The Doctor pointed at a small silver device on the neck of his suit.

Laura stared at him as if he was mad.

'That? A gravity inverter.'

The Doctor grinned. 'Don't tell the Cancri.'

Sincerely hoping that she had not opted to spend the last few moments of her life with a total madman, Laura had discarded her uniform jacket and belt, and started to pull on the spacesuit that the Doctor offered her.

Now she was standing in front of the strange old-fashioned doors as the Doctor made the final navigational adjustments to bring his ship alongside the alien wreck. The Doctor had deemed that attempting a landing inside the vessel came with too high a risk of shifting it from its precarious orbit or somehow alerting the Ba-El Cratt.

'Besides,' he had said with a grin. 'I thought that you might appreciate taking the scenic route.'

There was a slight jolt as the ship came to a standstill, and Laura was aware of a faint buzzing in her earpiece as the Doctor engaged the TARDIS force field.

He hurried over from the console. 'Ready?' he asked, looking for all the world like a small boy about to show off his latest toy.

Laura took a deep breath. 'Ready.'

The Doctor clicked his fingers and the door swung open.

And Laura stepped out onto the rings of Saturn.

Chapter

15

It was like every dream that Laura had ever had. No, she corrected herself. It was better than every dream she had ever had. Beneath her feet, the rings stretched off like a vast glittering highway, billions upon billions of tonnes of rock and ice slowly tumbling in an impossible ballet. Unable to quite believe that it was really happening, Laura took a step forwards, the sparkling energies of the force field that burst around her boots with every footfall making the experience even more surreal.

Aware that she was grinning like an idiot, Laura turned back towards the Doctor. He was just standing there, leaning casually against the side of the TARDIS, watching her. Laura couldn't help herself. She doubled over with laughter. It was so absurd. A man and his stupid blue box just hanging there against the huge boiling mass of the gas giant. She could feel tears rolling down her cheeks.

'Careful,' said the Doctor, walking forwards and catching her gently by the arm. 'Carry on like that and your helmet will fill up.'

The moment of hysteria passed and Laura blinked away the tears. 'Yeah. They didn't design these things for people who cry, sneeze or need to blow their nose.' She squeezed the Doctor's hand, the thick spacesuit gloves making the gesture clumsier than she would have liked. 'Thank you. For this.'

The Doctor gave the faintest of smiles. 'We should get on.'

With the Doctor leading the way, the two of them made their way along the force-field corridor towards the strange alien ship. As they approached, Laura could see long jagged gashes torn in the strange black material of the hull. Given the linear precision of the marks, it seemed unlikely that they had been caused naturally.

'Blaster damage?' she ventured.

The Doctor had obviously noted them too. 'Certainly caused by an energy weapon of some description.'

They reached the side of the ship and Laura reached out, running the palm of her glove of the pitted black surface. 'It looks like it's made of stone.'

'Or bone.'

'Bone?' Laura pulled her hand away in distaste.

'Yes.' The Doctor was starting up at the gentle curve of the spacecraft, lips pursed, eyes taking in every detail.

'The Alaskan Eskimos on Earth used to make their boats from whalebone. Funny how the same patterns occur throughout the universe.'

'You think that this is the skeleton of an animal of some kind?' Laura tried to take that in. 'But it's huge.'

'It's not unusual to find creatures from high-pressure planets growing to extreme sizes. If these animals have an exoskeleton capable of withstanding extreme pressures, then it stands to reason that they would be a useful resource. The Ba-El Cratt must possess an extremely sophisticated biomechanical technology.'

That was an understatement, thought Laura. It was no wonder that the ship hadn't shown up on sensors. There was nothing about its design or construction that would have registered as 'manufactured' in the traditional sense. She started to get a sensation of unease, wondering what else about the Ba-El Cratt was going to come as a surprise.

'Do you think that looks a likely candidate?'

The Doctor was leaning back, craning his neck to look at something high on the side of the ship. Laura followed his gaze. There was an opening in the hull, less haphazard than the huge raking gashes that they had already noticed. This looked more like an actual part of the ship. It was fairly obvious that the Doctor thought that this was an entrance of some kind.

Laura scanned the surface of the hull. Whilst it had initially looked completely smooth she could see that there were enough lumps, nodules and indentations to make the climb to the hole possible – tricky, but possible.

'I'm game if you are.'

'Come on, then.'

With no further ado, the Doctor started to make his way up the steep curve of the hull. Waiting a few moments until the Doctor had gained some height, Laura followed him, watching to see where he was finding suitable hand and footholds, and using the same points to aid her own ascent.

She had a sudden flashback to her time at the Academy, to the hours on the climbing wall that had formed part of her physical training. She could never have imagined that it would be perfect training for what she was doing now. Free climbing in the rings of Saturn. There was something for her memoirs. The difference was, back in the Academy there had always been the safety line to arrest her fall. If she slipped now, it was a one-way trip to the centre of the planet.

Then again, she mused, she might get lucky. She might get swept up amongst the tumbling boulders below and become part of the rings, gently orbiting for ever. Another 'Peggy'. That, she decided, would be a good way to go.

'This last bit is going to be tricky.'

The Doctor's voice snapped her from her daydream and she mentally scolded herself for getting so distracted. Above her, the Doctor was carefully navigating his way over the lip of the opening. Laura watched him nervously. The edges looked sharp. He could easily tear his suit open if he wasn't careful.

With a grunt of effort the Doctor hauled himself over the edge, vanishing inside the ship. Moments later he reappeared, peering down at her from the hole, the effort of the climb clearly visible on his face.

'Come on, I'll pull you up.' He reached out with a gloved hand to assist her.

Laura grasped his hand and, making sure that she kept her body well clear of the sharp edges, heaved herself into the fissure.

She found herself in a long, narrow passageway, totally dark and silent. The Doctor fumbled with something on his belt, and the interior of the ship was suddenly lit with a harsh, white light as the lamp on his helmet snapped on.

Laura gasped and took an involuntary step backwards, stumbling as the heel of her boot caught on the edge of the hole that she had just climbed through.

'Careful,' said the Doctor, pulling her away from the edge and turning on her own helmet light.

Nodding her thanks, Laura slowly made her forward, staring at the strange alien shapes that twisted around her. Any doubts that she had about the Doctor's theory that this ship might have once been a living creature were swiftly dispelled. The ship was so ... organic. It was if someone had given some lunatic artist a pile of bones and a bag of clay and asked him to make a sculpture.

'Come on, we'll try this way.' The Doctor set off along the corridor, seemingly unfazed by the strange biological nature of the vehicle. Not wanting to be left alone for one moment in this dark, unsettling place, Laura hurried after him.

'Bill?'

Bill's pent-up breath came out in a rush as she recognised the voice of Jo Teske. 'Oh, thank God. You gave me the fright of my life.'

Jo stared at her standing on the chair in bemusement. 'I was getting some stuff from my quarters. I saw the open door, heard someone inside … Bill, this is Rince's room, what on earth are you doing in here?'

Bill hopped down onto the floor, gabbling in her excitement. 'Jo, it's here. I think I've found it.'

'Found what?

'The transmitter, proof that Rince is the saboteur!'

'Transmitter? What transmitter?' Jo caught her by the shoulders. 'Bill, will you just slow down for one minute and tell me *what* you are talking about?'

Taking a deep breath, Bill explained about the ship in the rings, the crude way the communications system had been rigged to explode, the subspace signal that the Doctor had detected. From the expression on her face, Bill could tell that Jo was having trouble believing everything she was being told, but the proof she needed was literally at their feet.

Reluctantly, Jo had agreed to help her remove the panel from the ceiling, but after several minutes struggling with it, it became clear that it wasn't going to budge easily.

'It's no good, Bill. I agree that it *looks* like it can be moved, but it's obviously fixed somehow.'

Bill had to agree. 'If the Doctor was here he could probably move it in seconds with that sonic screwdriver of his.' A solution popped into her head. 'Graham's shed.'

'What?' Jo stared at her as if she was mad.

'Come on. We need to get some tools.'

The passageway that the Doctor and Laura were following suddenly opened up, the floor sloping away into a dark, oval chamber. Like the rest of the ship, the room was a weird juxtaposition of curving walls and jutting, bone-like structures.

'Ah, the control cabin,' said the Doctor, scurrying down the slope eagerly.

'And how exactly to you deduce that?' Laura hurried after him.

'Oh, pfff.' The Doctor waved a hand at her in irritation. 'I've been in enough bio-mechanical ships to recognise a control cabin when I see one. Zygon ships, Axon ships.

Even the TARDIS began life as a coral outgrowth, although I get the impression that she was never watered properly.'

'But …' Laura stared around the organic-looking space in bemusement. 'How? I mean where are the controls, the instruments …'

'Here.' The Doctor thrust his hand into one of the hundreds of indentations that pockmarked the walls, floor and ceiling of the chamber.

Laura peered into the hole. 'But there's nothing there. No circuitry. No connections.'

'You're still trying to make sense of this as if it's a recognisable piece of machinery.' The Doctor withdrew his hand from the hole and sighed. 'It's not your fault, I suppose. You do the best you can with those tiny little brains of yours.'

'Hey!'

Ignoring her look of indignation, the Doctor plucked at the fabric on the sleeve of her suit. 'Look, why do we wear these?'

'Because we need something that can sustain our atmosphere. Something that gives us protection against the cold, the radiation, the vacuum.'

'And if our suits are damaged?'

'We suffocate, we freeze, our blood boils.'

'Exactly! The pressure of our bodies has nothing outside to keep it in. Now, given everything that we've learned about the Ba-El Cratt they must be an aqueous life form of some kind.'

'Aqueous? You mean liquid?'

'Actually, I suspect that they are probably gelatinous, with a consistency similar to a very badly made blancmange, but my point is, think about what happens to a pressured liquid when you release it into a normal Earth-type atmosphere.'

Laura did think about it. If the Ba-El Cratt were a high-pressure liquid life form, then presumably they had to maintain that pressure in order to exist. Without it, the liquid in their makeup would turn to gas. They would literally evaporate into nothing. Explosively. 'It must make life very difficult.'

'It must make life virtually impossible!'

Laura looked around the chamber, trying to get her head around such a fundamentally different form of life. 'So you're saying that they just pour themselves into this … vessel?'

That made the Doctor grin. 'Exactly!' He walked to the middle of the chamber, throwing his arms wide and turning on a slow circle. 'This room would have been full to the brim with the crew. Just think about it, no connections, no communicators, no machinery, no technology, no shouting or yelling. Direct control. The entire crew, swimming around almost as if they were one creature, orders, conversations, instructions literally flowing between them.'

'And then they crashed.'

'Yes. In your solar system there are only three planets that they could possibly survive on, three gas giants that have the immense pressures that they need.'

'Then they took one hell of a risk in coming here.'

'Yes.' The Doctor looked thoughtful. 'I wonder why they did?'

Laura thought for a moment. 'Hang on, if they can only survive in extreme pressure then how come the ship is in orbit up here and they ended up down there?'

'Dunno.' The Doctor shrugged. 'I'm guessing that if we looked we'd find the equivalent of an escape pod missing.' His eyebrows suddenly twitched as a sudden thought stuck him. 'There must be a ship's log of some kind.'

Pulling his sonic screwdriver from a pouch in his suit, the Doctor started peering into the various holes and pits in the walls. Laura looked slowly around the room. It was beginning to seem ever more unlikely that Baines might be alive. Even if the Ba-El Cratt had managed to transport him up here somehow, there was no way that he could possibly survive in such an alien environment without his pressure armour.

An organic opening in the far wall caught her eye. If there was a chance – even a slim chance – that Baines was being kept prisoner in some other part of the ship then she had to at least look. She turned to let the Doctor know her intentions, but he was crouched down on the far side of the chamber, one arm reaching deep inside one of the larger openings, the green light from his sonic device casting a large flickering shadow of him on the ceiling.

Not wanting to disturb him, Laura made her way towards the opening and leaned through, the beam from her helmet lamp illuminating the narrow passageway beyond. Like the rest of the ship, the strange rib-like quality of the walls did nothing for Laura's nerves. It really was like being in the bowels of some enormous beast.

Cautiously, she started to make her way along the corridor, steadying herself against the wall as the ground underfoot became increasingly uneven. It suddenly struck her that in a vehicle where the crew literally filled up the interior like water in a fish tank she had no way of knowing if it was even the right way up or not. For all she knew she could be walking on the ceiling.

The corridor started to narrow, and Laura shot a nervous glance over her shoulder. The opening back out into the control cabin suddenly seemed a very long way away, and she began to doubt the wisdom of her decision to start exploring on her own. She closed her eyes, trying desperately to slow her pounding heart. This was ridiculous, she told herself angrily. She was a highly trained Federation security officer.

'So act like one,' she muttered under her breath. 'Not like some teenager in a haunted house.'

She trained her helmet light on the passageway ahead. The twisting alien shapes made it difficult to judge distance properly, but it looked as though the corridor came to an abrupt end only a few metres ahead of her. She started to move forward once more. If it did turn out to be a dead end, she would just turn around and go back.

As she neared the end of the passageway she became aware that it too opened out, in a similar way to the one leading into the control room. This chamber was far, far smaller, however. And there, in the far corner, there seemed to be something scattered on the floor.

She turned her head, trying to train the beam from her helmet onto the objects to get a better look. As the light panned across them, Laura felt a chill of horror grip her. At the same moment, she suddenly became aware of something crashing along the corridor behind her.

She spun, arms raised to ward off her attacker, only to see the Doctor's panic-stricken face staring at her, condensation from his laboured breathing clouding the visor of his helmet. 'We have to get back to the rig,' he gasped 'Right now.'

'Wait!' Laura shouted as he tried to turn around in the narrow passageway. 'Doctor, I think this might be Baines.'

Laura stepped aside, allowing the light from the Doctor's helmet torch to shine onto what she had found.

Bones, lots of them, the skull staring blankly from amongst them clearly humanoid in origin.

The Doctor hurried forwards, kneeling down and scanning the pathetic pile of remains with his sonic screwdriver. 'No, it's not Baines,' said the Doctor grimly. 'There is more than one body here. And they're not human.'

'Then who …?'

'They're Cancri.' The Doctor stared up at her. 'The aliens that the Ba-El Cratt are at war with are the Cancri.'

Chapter

16

Standing in front of the workbench in the equipment room, Bill could have screamed with frustration. Unlike the canteen, where she had found everything boringly familiar, here she could see nothing that even vaguely resembled a wrench or a screwdriver.

Jo was just watching her from the doorway.

'Well, come on,' said Bill impatiently. 'Help me look for something that we can use to get that ceiling panel down.'

Jo gave deep sigh. Bill could tell that the medic was rapidly starting to think that this was a waste of time. 'Bill, this is crazy. Just go to Delitsky and tell him what you suspect.'

'I can't. Not yet.' Bill already knew that with the Doctor unhelpfully not around, she was going to need hard evidence if Delitsky was going to take anything she said seriously. The transmitter was the only hard evidence she had. 'Jo, please?'

'All right, all right.' Jo joined her at the workbench. 'What is it you need?'

'I don't know. A screwdriver of some kind. Or a spanner.'

Jo peered at the cluttered workbench. 'Can't see anything here.'

'I can see that. Why don't you try that tool cupboard?'

Without enthusiasm, Jo wandered over to the metal tool cupboard standing at the end of the bench. 'It's Jenloz's.'

'How can you tell?'

Jo indicated the cluster of strange, almost Arabic letters stencilled in yellow paint across the door. 'That's his name in Cancri. He's been trying to teach me to read it all year.' She tried the handle. 'It's locked.'

'Here.' Bill tossed her the bundle of electronic keys. 'Try those.'

Jo caught them. 'Aren't these ...?'

'Don't ask!'

As Jo started to try the different security keys in the lock, Bill ducked down under the workbench, dragging out a couple of toolboxes that had been stashed there. They too were locked. She was about to ask for the keys, when there was a sudden cry of dismay, following by a deafening crash.

Bill scrambled to her feet. Jo had succeeded in unlocking the tool cupboard, but in doing so had dislodged the pile of tools that had obviously been precariously balanced behind the door. She'd made quite a mess, but amongst the chaos Bill could see exactly what she was after.

'Jackpot.'

She hurried forward to grab one of the spanners that lay scattered across the floor, but in her haste, tripped on something small and metallic which sent her sprawling.

'Ow!'

'Are you OK?' Jo helped her back onto her feet.

'Yeah, just wasn't looking where I was stepping.'

Bill looked down to see what it was that she had tripped over. As she reached out for the object, she felt a sudden chill of dread.

'Oh no …'

'What is it?'

Bill held out the object for Jo to see. It was a tight bundle of complex-looking electronic circuitry, the loose wires and connectors making it clear that it was a part that had been removed from some larger mechanism. Part of the metal casing was painted a vibrant cherry red. It was the pressure controller that had been removed from Baines's suit. The two women stared at it for a moment, then turned in unison to look at the name stencilled in Cancri script on the door of the tool cupboard.

'Jenloz,' breathed Jo.

Bill nodded, realising that she had unwittingly managed to unmask not just one of the saboteurs, but both of them.

Jo's eyes widened in horror as she suddenly remembered what it was that the Chief Engineer was currently doing.

'The depressurisation chamber. Bill, he's going to try and kill the others!'

The Doctor raced back through main corridor leading from the control cabin, his bulky spacesuit making his long-limbed gait seem even more ungainly than usual. Laura was barely able to keep pace with him.

'This ship isn't marooned in the rings, it's been left here deliberately,' he bellowed.

'But the Ba-El Cratt said they had crashed. That they were stranded.'

'And they lied. Just like they lied about Baines. They wanted to gain your trust. What better way than to play at being helpless refugees.'

'But how do you *know*?' yelled Laura.

'I managed to access a navigational log. Not easy when it's only really designed to be accessed by a sentient high-pressure, semi-gelatinous life form but, you know, genius.'

Laura could have hit him. Even at times like this he still needed to show off. 'Will you stop being so smug and just tell me what you found!'

'The ship was steered into Saturn. A pre-programmed trajectory that allowed the Ba-El Cratt to bail out when they were at a safe depth. The ship then regained altitude and went into orbit in the rings, powering down all its systems so that it could hide there undetected.'

'But why strand themselves like that?' asked Laura, as they arrived at the opening in the hull.

'Because the atmosphere of Saturn is a close match to the natural environment these creatures need to survive. It's impossible for you to reach without significant amounts of technology, and electrically unstable enough for them to be able to evade any sensors that might possibly be able to detect them. Plus I'm assuming that they have the ability to recall their ship at any point if they need to evacuate.'

The Doctor was already halfway out of the opening, and starting to make his descent down the hull. Realising that he had no intention of helping her through, Laura scrambled after him.

'But why?'

'They've been studying you. Waiting for the right moment to make their move. I'm guessing they've been there for weeks. They've been able to survive quite happily in Saturn's atmosphere, and that's given them plenty of time to work out that they could use the miners' pressure armour to survive in *your* atmosphere.'

The Doctor leapt from the hull, the force field cracking ferociously as his boots made contact with it. He raced towards the TARDIS, and Laura suddenly had the horrible impression that he might not wait for her if she didn't get a move on. Pushing off from the hull, she jumped the last metre and a half, landing on her knees with an impact that nearly winded her.

She scrambled to her feet and sprinted forwards, hurling herself through the open doors and into the control room beyond. The Doctor had already discarded his space helmet and was dancing around the console, flicking at switches like a man possessed.

As Laura struggled with the clasp on her own helmet, the doors slammed shut behind her, and that strange, rasping grind of engines reverberated around the room as the TARDIS took flight.

Gasping, Laura let the helmet drop from her fingers and it clattered across the floor. Wincing at the pain from her bruised knees, she limped across the room towards the Doctor. His face was grim.

'OK,' said Laura, trying to catch her breath, 'Let's say you're right about all this. It still doesn't necessarily mean that they pose any immediate threat. They've made no hostile action towards us.'

'And how do you think they'll react when they realise that the rig – your entire mining operation – is run in partnership with the Cancri, hmm? You said that you didn't want to find yourself in the middle of a war. Well, that ship out there in the rings is an assault craft, a very sophisticated assault craft, and if the Ba-El Cratt see you as *allies* of the Cancri, then a war might be just what you get.'

An alarm started to sound on the console, and the Doctor turned towards it in dismay.

'Oh no …'

'What is it?'

The Doctor stabbed at a control. As the monitor screen came to life all colour drained from Laura's face, and she slumped back against one of the handrails that ran around the console room.

'Oh, my God.'

On the screen, Kollo-Zarnista Mining Facility 27 was slowly sinking into the clouds of Saturn, gouts of flame and debris trailing from a dark, ragged hole in the hull.

'I think that the war might already have started,' said the Doctor.

Chapter

17

At any other time, the TARDIS materialising in the corner of the control room might have caused consternation, but at the moment no one even bothered to give it a second look. Even the sound of the materialisation was drowned out by the combination of screaming voices and blaring sirens. Everyone was too busy just trying to stay alive.

One person did notice its arrival, however, and dashed forward as the doors swung open and the Doctor and Laura emerged.

'Doctor!' Bill had never been so glad to see him in her life. To his surprise (and, she had to admit, to hers as well), she threw her arms around him and gave him a hug of relief. 'You know, I was beginning to think you might have got lost.'

The Doctor disentangled himself from her embrace. He looked embarrassed. 'Are you OK?'

'What happened?' Laura stared around the chaos of the control room in shock.

'Jenloz.' Jo Teske had noted their arrival too. She exchanged a momentary glance with Laura. Her eyes flicked from the security officer to the police box and back again. They were going to have a lot to discuss later. If they survived this, that was.

'What did he do?' asked the Doctor urgently.

'Sabotaged the decompression chamber in the med-bay. A small explosive device, as far as we can tell.'

'Small?' Laura steadied herself against the TARDIS as the dull 'crump' of other distant explosion rocked the station.

'Two of the Ba-El Cratt were inside the chamber at the time,' explained Jo. 'Their suits must have been damaged by the initial blast ...'

'And there was a massive explosive decompression.'

Jo nodded. 'Took the medical bay and a fair chunk of the outer hull with them.' Her face was grim. 'And about six of the crew.'

'And you're sure it was Jenloz?' asked Palmer.

Bill nodded. 'We found the missing pressure regulator from the first sabotage attempt in his locker.'

Palmer shot a glance at the Doctor. 'That confirms that, then ...'

'We also found that secret transmitter.'

'Secret transmitter?' Palmer frowned. 'What secret transmitter?'

'We haven't got time to worry about that now,' snapped the Doctor. 'I've got everyone on this station to save.'

Locating Delitsky amongst the chaos, the Doctor hurried to his side. The Rig Chief and his crew were working frantically at the controls, doing their best to try and stabilise the crippled mining platform and stop its doomed decent into the atmosphere. As far as the Doctor could tell, they weren't succeeding.

'Ah, there you are.' Delitsky didn't look up. 'Nice of you to finally join us.'

'Been busy.' The Doctor's eyes were roaming all across the console, taking in every setting, ever readout. 'Can I help?'

Delitsky gave a humourless laugh. 'Be my guest. At this point I'm open to any suggestions.' From the tone of his voice, it was clear that he thought that they were past saving.

The Doctor glanced at the panel monitoring the gravity inverters and frowned. The Cancri machines appeared to be undamaged; they just weren't doing their job properly.

'Your gravity inverters are slipping out of phase. Why aren't they synchronising?'

'Because the explosion took out a major cable run. I've got a repair crew there, but …' Delitsky shrugged. 'It's a lot of damage. They'll never get it done in time.'

'Can you reroute?'

'That's what we're trying. I've got Robbins sending data via the internal comms system. But the network just doesn't have the capacity to shunt the data fast enough.'

The Doctor's mind was racing. The gravity inverters worked by keeping in sync with each other, monitoring the mass of the station millisecond-by-millisecond, and readjusting the anti-gravity settings accordingly. Breaking the connection between the four machines had caused an imbalance.

Four machines …

'Balls …'

Delitsky stared at him. 'What?'

'Balls!' The Doctor hurried across to the control room to Palmer. 'Those robots of yours … What did you call them? The Flying Squad?'

She nodded. 'Uh, huh.'

'Get them up here.'

'Now?' Laura looked confused.

'Now!'

Such was the urgency in the Doctor's voice that Laura didn't bother to argue. She turned to an emergency alarm on the wall and punched out the glass. Immediately a new siren joined the cacophony in the control room.

Pulling the sonic screwdriver from his pocket the Doctor turned, and waited. Moments later, the four silver security robots burst from their launch tubes and hovered, buzzing, in the centre of the control room.

'Ah, there we are. John, Paul, George and Ringo. I've a little job for you boys.' The Doctor turned back to Laura. 'I need a master voice command override.'

Laura looked startled. 'I can't do that.'

'You must.'

'I can't. It breaks every rule, every regulation. It would be the end of my career ...'

'Your career?' The Doctor gave a sharp barking laugh. 'Your career is going to end as a compressed speck in the centre of Saturn, and the careers of everyone else on this station are going to end the same way, unless you give me control of these robots.'

She stared at him, the conflict clear on her face.

'Listen.' The Doctor's voice had dropped to a whisper. 'I can save the lives of everyone here. Every. Single. One. I know how to get the gravity inverters back on line, I know how to get this rig back into its correct orbit, but I need those robots to do it. If you won't help, then ...'

As if to confirm what he was saying, the rig gave an ominous creak as the hull was squeezed ever tighter by Saturn's crushing grip. Whether it was because of the Doctor's words, or the noise from outside, Laura took a deep breath, and looked up at the hovering robots.

'This is Captain Laura J. Palmer, Federation Security Officer for Kollo-Zarnista Mining Facility 27, badge number 047-K1Z. Verify voice print.'

There was a series of electronic burbles from each of the robots.

'Initiate command override. Confirm.'

The robots gave another burble of confirmation, and a green light lit up on each of their casings.

Laura stepped back and raised an arm towards the hovering spheres. 'They're all yours.'

Rubbing his hands together in eagerness, the Doctor bustled forward. 'Right, lads. First thing I need to you to do is locate all that boring criminal law in your data banks and delete it. Every last piece. You're going to need the memory space.'

Laura Palmer had to bite her lip.

'I'm assuming that each of these robots is capable of interfacing with other terminals on the station?' asked the Doctor.

'Standard positronic adaptor.'

'Right.' The Doctor scampered back to the main control console and started making adjustments with his sonic screwdriver. He was still giving instructions to the robots. 'As soon as you've done that, clear your communications channels and stand by for priority command. I'm going to give you some proper work to do!' He spun to face Delitsky. 'Now, I need Jenloz down here.'

The Rig Chief opened his mouth to complain, but before he could utter a word the Doctor held up a spindly finger to silence him.

'The gravitic calculations that are needed to bring the inverters back into phase are incredibly complex. I am more than capable of doing them but, much as it pains me to admit it, Jenloz will be much, much faster. Now, do I need to give you the same speech that I just gave Officer Palmer or will you just trust me and do what I ask?'

Delitsky reached up and tapped his ear bud. 'Sergeant Harrison, will you please bring the Chief Engineer down to main control. On the double.'

Bill watched the Doctor as he worked at incredible speed. It looked to her as if he was completely rebuilding the computer, darting from console to console, stopping for a moment to peer at a bewildering selection of complicated schematics on various screens before returning to the main control panel and delving inside it, pulling out wires and replacing circuitry. All the while he kept issuing a stream of precise instructions to the waiting robots.

He didn't even look up from his work when Jenloz was marched into the control room and pushed into the chair alongside him.

'He can't do the work in handcuffs,' snapped the Doctor, using his sonic screwdriver to make yet another delicate adjustment.

At a nod from Delitsky, Harrison reached down and released the restraints from the little Cancri's wrists.

The Doctor slid a keyboard in front of him. 'I need you to upload the gravitic equations to the security robots,' he explained calmly. 'Their emergency command structure is more than capable of handling the data stream needed to bring the inverters back into sync and stabilise this rig.'

Jenloz didn't move. Bill held her breath, waiting to see what the Doctor would do.

'My guess is that you didn't intend for the explosion to be as big as it was. Your plan was to destroy the pressure chamber and kill as many of the Ba-El Cratt as you could. But you didn't account for the effect of their explosive decompression, did you?'

Still the engineer said nothing.

'I know that you consider yourself to be a soldier, and that the action you took was somehow justified, but your war is not with the people here in this room, the crew that you have worked with on this rig. I don't really know if it matters to you whether I think you are a soldier or not. But I don't think you're a murderer.'

Bill let out her breath in a gasp as Jenloz reached for the keyboard, and began to type. As calculations began to cascade across the monitor screens, the Doctor raised his sonic screwdriver like a conductor about to begin a concerto.

A horrible wrenching screech suddenly shattered the petrified silence in the control room, forcing Bill to clap her hands over her ears. There were screams of terror as the crew and she realised, with a sudden moment of helpless resignation, that the rig was finally at the point where it could no longer resist the grip that Saturn had on it.

At the very same moment Jenloz finished his calculations and, as Bill watched, he turned to the Doctor and gave him a solemn nod.

'All right, fellas. Let's go!' shouted the Doctor.

There was an electronic burble from the screwdriver, and Bill ducked as each of the robots shot off in a different direction at incredible speed.

The Doctor hunched down over the monitor screen. Craning her neck, Bill could see the schematic of the station showing the progress of the robots as they raced through the infrastructure of station towards the four gravity inverters on its outer edge.

She gritted her teeth as another protesting groan came from the hull and the entire station shuddered.

'She's going to break up!' gasped Delitsky, watching over the Doctor's shoulder. 'Doctor, she's going to break up!'

Bill's heart was pounding

'Come on, come on …'

She could hear the Doctor's voice as he willed the robots onwards. Each of them was closing rapidly on its destination, but was it too late?

'Almost there … Almost …'

A look of triumph flashed across the Doctor's face as, across the board, indicator lights went green as the robots reached the gravity inverters and interfaced with the system controls. The Doctor stabbed at a control and there was a sudden whine of power as the systems started to reintegrate.

The effect on the station was immediate. The vibration that had threatened to shake the teeth from Bill's head finally subsided, and a gentle background hum took its place. Alarms suddenly cut off, leaving the control room uncannily quiet.

Delitsky was staring in disbelief at his controls. 'She's stabilising. No, wait … she's lifting! She's actually lifting!'

The Rig Chief slumped back into his chair, as the room erupted into exciting cheering. People were crowding around the Doctor, shaking him by the hand and thumping him on the back. Bill pushed her way through them to his side.

'You did it!'

He glared at her indignantly. 'Of course I did it. I'm the Doctor.'

At any other time, Bill might have rolled her eyes and told him to stop being so big-headed, but given that he had just saved the lives of every person on the rig, she'd let him off.

'Of course you are. Sorry, I was forgetting.'

A sudden movement on the far side of the control room caught her eye, and she frowned as one of the surviving Ba-El Cratt in its borrowed pressure armour stamped into the room. Another followed, and Bill's eyes widened in alarm as she realised that they both had g-Tasers grasped in their huge hands.

As more and more people became aware of the lumbering figures, the excited chatter in the control room faded, to be replaced with an uneasy silence.

The third of the Ba-El Cratt entered the room, pushing Officer Sillitoe in front of him. From the look of pain on the security officer's face, and the way that he was holding his arm, it seemed obvious that he and the rest of his team had not surrendered their weaponry without a struggle.

'What is the meaning of this?' Delitsky scrambled from his seat. 'Officer Sillitoe, what's happening?'

'Sorry, Chief,' Sillitoe gasped. 'They jumped us, clubbed a couple of the guys unconscious and took their g-Tasers. I tried to stop them but ...'

He broke off, obviously in considerable pain. Jo Teske scurried across to control room towards him, but one of the Ba-El Cratt swung around its g-Taser to point at her.

'You will all stand still.' The hissing voice boomed around the room. 'This facility is now under the command of the Ba-El Cratt Collective.'

'His arm is obviously broken.' Jo yelled angrily. 'I need to help him.'

'He tried to resist us. That was foolish. If he attempts to do so again, we will kill him.'

'Why?' snapped Delitsky angrily. 'You came here asking for help and we have given it. What possible reason could you have for doing this?'

'Two of us are dead.'

'That was not of our doing.' Delitsky pointed across the room at Jenloz. 'This man—'

'This man is a Cancri.' Even through the speakers of the suit the venom was evident in the Ba-El Cratt's voice. 'And you are right, it is he who is guilty of causing the deaths of my brothers. But you have chosen to ally yourselves with them, to assist in their war against us.'

'That's not true, we—'

'Silence!' roared the huge figure. 'Your collaboration with his species has helped bring about the destruction of hundreds of thousands of my kind.'

Delitsky went pale. 'Hundreds of thousands ... How?'

'Because of the diamonds.' The Doctor's voice cut across the shocked silence in the control room.

'Yes,' hissed the Ba-El Cratt. 'Because of your assistance in the Cancri weapons programme.'

'Weapons?' floundered Delitsky. 'You mean the Cancri are buying weapons with the diamonds?'

'No. I'm guessing that the diamonds are actually a vital part of the Cancri weapons,' said the Doctor. 'Presumably they are using them as some kind of Raman

Amplification system in a projected energy weapon of some description.'

The Doctor's explanation was just so much scientific gobbledegook as far as Bill was concerned, but it certainly brought him to the attention of the Ba-El Cratt.

'Correct. Over the many years that the war has raged, both sides have become ever more efficient at creating protective armour. Now only weaponry that utilises crystalline carbon focusing arrays is effective. We thought that we had destroyed all Cancri diamond production facilities in our system. We soon realised that they must have an alternative source elsewhere. And an ally to assist them … By association you too have declared war on the Ba-El Cratt, and you all share their guilt. You will also share their fate.' The Ba-El Cratt leader pointed at Jenloz. 'But he will be first.'

Showing uncommon bravery, Delitsky stepped in front of Jenloz, his arms outstretched. 'This man is part of my crew and is subject to our laws. If he has committed a crime against you then he will be punished but we will do it in our way.'

'I am not interested in your primitive laws. He has been found guilty. He will die now.'

The other two Ba-El Cratt started to lurch forward, but the Doctor suddenly launched himself forwards, vaulting over the console and landing between them and the terrified Cancri engineer.

'No,' said the Doctor firmly. 'I'm afraid I cannot allow that.'

'Cannot allow?' snarled the Ba-El Cratt.

'No, sorry.' The Doctor stared up at the huge figure. 'Look, can I ask who am I addressing? I mean I'm terribly old-fashioned. I like names. I can't start referring to you as "the Big Red Stompy One", can I?'

'Names mean nothing. We are the Ba-El Cratt. We are as one. We fight as one. We die as one.'

The Doctor shrugged. 'Stompy it is then. Well, you claim that you are at war with the Cancri. If that's the case, then there are rules. Murder is not one of those rules. I invoke Article Fifteen of the Shadow Proclam—'

Before the Doctor could finish speaking, the Ba-El Cratt leader raised its g-Taser and blasted him and Delitsky at point-blank range.

Chapter

18

Bill looked down at the Doctor's expressionless face, willing him to wake up. Alongside her, Jo Teske was doing her best to revive Delitsky. Both of them had been unconscious for several minutes. Bill considered them the lucky ones.

The gravity pulse fired by the Ba-El Cratt leader had hurled both men across the control room, sending them crashing against the wall. As people had rushed forward to help them, the other two Ba-El Cratt had grabbed hold of Jenloz and dragged him into the middle of the room. Their leader had joined them, and all three had surrounded the diminutive engineer.

'For crimes committed against the Ba-El Cratt, I order your immediate execution.'

Jenloz had just stared up at them defiantly, clasping his fist over his chest in salute. 'For Cancri.'

Then – and Bill could still not get this image out of her head – all three of the Ba-El Cratt had begun to move, tightening the circle around Jenloz, the metal of their pressure armour screeching and scraping as they pushed tighter and tighter together.

Bill knew that the noises that followed would probably stay in her nightmares for a very long time.

Their brutal execution complete, the Ba-El Cratt had stepped apart, and Jenloz's mangled body fell to the floor.

Ignoring the screams of horror and revulsion, the three armoured figures had ushered the bulk of the crew into the hangar bay, sealing the pressure doors, and warning of the consequences for everyone if any attempt to escape was made. A few unlucky individuals had been kept back by the Ba-El Cratt to assist them. Through the hangar bay windows, Bill could see them at their consoles, studiously keeping their eyes from straying to the tiny broken corpse that had been left on the floor.

'What are they doing?' hissed Nettleman, his eyes wild and staring. As far as Bill could tell, he was on the point of totally losing it.

'They're prepping the vault,' said Laura, her head cocked on one side. 'I can hear the big cargo shifters powering up.'

'The diamonds?' Nettleman croaked. 'They're going to take the diamonds? But they need a ship …'

'Oh, they've got a ship,' Laura pointed out grimly. 'And it's probably already on its way.'

There was a groan from the Doctor, and his eyes started to flicker open.

'Jo.' Bill waved her over. 'He's coming round.'

The two of them helped the Doctor to sit up, leaning him back against the hangar wall.

'Take it slowly,' said Jo, examining him carefully. 'You were hit at close range with a gravity-Taser. You're going to be groggy for a while. You're lucky it wasn't at full power.'

'Delitsky?' The Doctor rubbed at his eyes.

On cue, there was a moan of discomfort from the Rig Chief. Jo scurried over to him. 'He'll be fine. He'll have one hell of a headache, but other than that …'

'And Jenloz?'

Jo dropped her gaze.

'They killed him,' said Bill quietly.

The Doctor's face hardened and, ignoring Jo's protests, he struggled to his feet. 'What are they doing now?' he asked, swaying somewhat drunkenly as he tried to regain his balance.

'They've started the automatic loading procedure,' explained Laura. 'It's usually triggered when the mine reaches capacity. A high-security freighter is sent from Earth or Cancri and loaded with the cylinders in the vault. New empty cylinders are delivered and the mine starts filling them up again.'

'And how long does this process usually take?' asked the Doctor, still teetering slightly.

Laura shrugged. 'Once they've managed to dock their ship, it could be less than thirty minutes. It's one of the most vulnerable parts of the entire operation so the automatics are designed to be pretty quick.'

'Then we don't have much time.' The Doctor spun to face Bill. 'So Jenloz turned out to be one of our saboteurs. Who was the other?'

Bill pointed to where Rince was sitting forlornly on a crate in the middle of the hangar. 'Him.'

Every face turned towards the Kollo-Zarnista executive.

'Rince?' Nettleman's jaw was hanging open in disbelief.

Laura Palmer was equally incredulous. 'Are you saying that *he* was responsible for wrecking the communications console? Surely Jenloz …'

'Jenloz was a highly trained engineer. There are a million ways he could have disabled the communications grid if he wanted to without having to resort to anything as crude as the solution that our friend here tried.' The Doctor pulled up a crate and sat down opposite Rince. 'No, that was an act of desperation because Delitsky was going to call in the cavalry, and the arrival of armed guards would really not have gone down well with your pirate chums, would it?'

'Pirates?' Nettleman's voice was practically a squeak.

'Pirates. Buccaneers. Gem Raiders. Soldiers of Fortune. Call them whatever you want, the point is they're out there, and they're waiting for the word from their man on the inside.'

Rince looked at him wearily. 'You've worked it all out, haven't you?'

'All except why.'

'He's why.' Rince pointed accusingly at Nettleman.

'Me?' Nettleman shook his head. 'Don't you dare bring me into this.'

'Oh, what's the point, Donald? It's over. Don't you see? We're going to die, so there's no point in pretending any more.' Rince gave a deep sigh. 'All of the recent diamond thefts have been orchestrated by me, under direction from Senior Executive Nettleman.'

'Rince,' snarled Nettleman. 'Be quiet.'

'Oh, will someone shut him up!' snapped the Doctor. He turned back to Rince. 'Why?'

'Because the Kollo-Zarnista Mining Company has a massive black hole in its pension fund. A black hole that Nettleman has been keeping quiet from the rest of the board because it has been his misappropriation of those funds, and a subsequent run of bad luck at the Olympus Mons Casino, that has caused it.' The confession tumbled from Rince's lips; he was obviously tired of keeping so many secrets and glad to finally have a chance to unburden himself. 'Nettleman came up with a plan to gradually replace the missing funds by removing a small quantity of diamonds from each Cancri-bound shipment and selling them off through the black market. My job was to ensure that the books balanced, hiding the fact that the diamonds were being siphoned off.'

'So what went wrong?'

Rince shrugged. 'Carelessness on my part. A lapse of concentration. Nettleman got scared that we weren't replacing the missing funds fast enough. He wanted to increase the quantity of diamonds that we were stealing. I made a mistake in the book-keeping, the Cancri noticed, so head office started an inquiry.'

'And Nettleman made sure that he was put in charge of that inquiry.'

Rince nodded. 'At first I thought that was perfect. No one suspected him, so I figured we'd easily be able to put things right. Then I started to realise exactly how he operates.'

Rince looked across at his boss, his dislike for the man plain to see. 'He surrounds himself with people he can point to as the cause when anything that *he* does goes wrong. I thought that with him leading the investigation I'd be safe. What I was really doing was setting myself up to take the blame.'

'So you came up with a plan of your own.'

Rince nodded. 'I knew the diamond shipment schedules backwards, I knew the security protocols, I knew the transponder codes…'

'You betrayed me!' spat Nettleman.

'*I* betrayed *you*?' gasped Rince in disbelief. 'You were getting ready to throw me to the wolves. I knew that you had a reputation for finding other people on your team to take the fall for you, but I was naive enough to think that it would be different this time. That we were partners. It was only when I hacked your personal server …'

'You hacked me?' Nettleman looked outraged.

'Oh, come on. You were quite happy to use me to break into the company mainframe to do your dirty work. Did you really think that I wouldn't also check up on you, just to make sure that you were playing fair? Well, guess what, Donald? You weren't.'

'And you thought that hooking up with pirates was the best option you had?' Bill raised an eyebrow. 'Bit of an overreaction!'

'You think so? Attempting to defraud a Federation-backed diamond franchise isn't something that ends with a smack on the wrist and a note on your personal file. It ends with you being shipped off to one of the penal colonies, and I really have no intention of spending the rest of my life digging ore on Cygnus-A or Varos.'

'So these friends of yours, these pirates. They're waiting for a signal from you, correct?' From the urgency in his voice, Bill could tell that the Doctor was starting to come up with a plan.

Rince nodded. 'If everything had gone to plan, Nettleman and I would have completed our investigations here with the conclusion that security on this mine was substandard and in need of total overhaul. We would then have recommended the immediate shipment of the diamonds back to Earth and Cancri. During the loading procedure, my job was to doctor the records to make it look as though the source of the diamond theft was here, covering up for my earlier blunder.' He shot a look at Nettleman. 'It seems that what was actually going to happen is that I was going to be caught in the act, making him the hero of the hour.'

'So you planned to get the entire shipment stolen instead.'

'I met a woman who said she could provide a ship and a way out if I could get her the inside information she needed. It seemed like a good plan.'

'He'd still have been able to pin the blame on you,' Bill pointed out. 'You'd still never have been able to go back to Earth.'

'No.' Rince shrugged. 'That's true, but a least I'd have a fortune in diamonds, and there are enough planets in the outer colonies where you can be comfortable. If you're rich enough.'

'So this heist.' The Doctor was getting impatient now. 'How was it going to work?'

'The diamond freighter used a sensor-scattering array to stop any ship getting a clear lock on it. That can't be disabled. I know – I tried. So, instead I was to place a subspace transponder inside one of the diamond strongboxes. When that box was loaded onto the ship ...'

'The pirates would be able to get a sensor lock.'

'I'd already given them the access codes to the airlocks. From the timing simulations that we ran it looked as though they should have been able to get on board, take the diamonds and escape before the security teams realised what was happening.'

'So they are just waiting for you to tell them that the freighter is on its way to Earth and for you to give them the frequency of the subspace transponder?'

'Yes.'

'Excellent!' The Doctor seemed very happy with the information. Bill couldn't work out why.

'I don't see how that helps us,' she said. 'The freighter isn't here, and the transponder is in his cabin.'

'But the pirates are still out there,' said the Doctor.

Any explanation he might have been about to give was halted as the door to the hangar hissed open and one of the Ba-El Cratt lumbered into the room.

'Oh, look, it's Stompy,' cried the Doctor cheerfully. 'How's the diamond theft going? You seem to be having better luck than I did. All sorts of alarms went off when I tried it. Not my fault of course. That was down to my pudding brain of an assistant …'

'Silence!' bellowed the Ba-El Cratt. 'Your endless prattling serves no purpose. Thankfully I shall not have to listen to it much longer. As soon as our ship is re-pressurised …'

'Oh!' The Doctor regarded the alien carefully. 'Don't tell me that you're leaving already? You only just arrived.'

'Our mission was only ever meant to be one of intelligence gathering. The capture and interrogation of a Cancri raiding party had alerted us to the fact that they had another source of diamonds far beyond our system. We were to locate the source of those diamonds, and to learn who was assisting them. We have successfully completed that mission. The acquisition of the diamonds from your mine is an additional bonus. One that will greatly assist our own war effort.'

'So that's it, you're just going to take the diamonds and fly off?' Delitsky couldn't keep the disbelief from his voice. 'Right.'

'You have assisted the Cancri, and that will not stand without retaliation,' said the Ba-El Cratt leader menacingly. 'But I am not so foolish as to embark on a war against an entire species with the remnants of one commando squad and a single assault craft.'

'So you're off to get reinforcements,' said the Doctor grimly.

'And when we return, we will annihilate this and every other mine.'

'You cannot do this,' yelled Delitsky. 'We are not part of your war.'

'Oh, but you are.'

'Then we will fight,' said Laura coldly.

'Yes,' hissed the Ba-El Cratt. 'I know you will.' The creature turned, raised an armoured glove and pointed at Bill. 'Put her into a pressure suit.'

'What?' Bill stared in surprise. 'Me?'

The Doctor caught hold of her arm reassuringly. 'Why?'

'As insurance.'

'Against what?'

'I am not a fool, Doctor. The moment we leave, you will attempt to stop our ship. Its function requires three of us. Our intention had been to leave two of our number on board this station, but the hostile actions taken against us force us to use different means of dissuasion. If any aggressive action is taken against us, the girl will die.'

'No.' The Doctor stepped forward, shielding her. 'She's just a child. If you want a hostage take me instead.'

'No.'

'Why not?'

'Because you wish it.' The creature pointed its g-Taser at the Doctor's chest. 'I have shown leniency towards you once, Doctor. Don't rely on that happening a second time.'

Face darkening, the Doctor stepped towards the Ba-El Cratt leader. 'Let me remind you of something. You owe your life to me.' He stretched out a finger, pointing at the repairs that he had made to the pressure regulator on the armoured suit. 'Without me, your armour would have depressurised, your mission would have failed and you would be nothing more than dissipated gas. Everything that you are doing here, any glory that you hope to gain, is only possible because I helped you to survive.'

Bill held her breath as the Ba-El Cratt leader regarded the Doctor silently for what seemed like forever, but could only really have been a matter of seconds. Then it lowered its weapon.

'Put him in a suit instead.'

Delitsky and Jo Teske helped the Doctor clamber into the huge suit of pressure armour and started to hook him into the controls. Bill stood to one side watching them nervously.

'Are you sure that this is a good idea, Doctor?' muttered Delitsky. 'Once you're on board that ship and it's undocked, we've no way of getting you back.'

'You let me worry about how to get back, Chief Delitsky. If I'm right, then once that ship undocks you're going to have more than enough problems of your own.'

Delitsky grunted in agreement. There wasn't a single member of his crew that believed that the Ba-El Cratt were going to just fly off into the sunset leaving everyone unharmed. They had already shown such a casual disregard for life that it wasn't a question of if the rig was going to be destroyed; it was a question of when and how.

'Why is this taking so long?' boomed the voice of the waiting Ba-El Cratt. 'We must leave, now.'

'He's not getting measured for a dress suit, you know,' snapped Delitsky. 'This is a complex piece of survival equipment, and it takes time to prepare.'

'It is primitive and inefficient,' hissed the creature. 'Like so much that the Cancri creates. Now stop delaying and finish your work.'

'Lovely motivational style they have,' said the Doctor under his breath.

'Yeah.' Delitsky gave a snort of agreement. 'You'd imagine that they'd get on well with Nettleman.'

The levity faded from the Doctor's voice. 'How's Bill?'

Delitsky shot her a quick glance. Bill returned his gaze with the briefest of nods.

'She's good.'

'Right then. Turn me on.'

Jo Teske keyed in the start-up sequence that would allow the Doctor to activate the armour, and he made a theatrical show of stretching the arms and operating the claws.

'All connections green.' Delitsky tried to keep his voice sounding natural. 'Ready to pressurise.'

Bill suddenly ran forward, pushing past Jo and throwing herself against the front of the armoured suit. 'Doctor, please,' she pleaded. 'You can't do this to me. If anything happens to you then I'm stuck here!'

'I've no choice.' The Doctor wouldn't meet her gaze.

'Well, why does it have to be you? Why can't you let someone else go in your place?'

He looked up, a thin smile on his lips. 'Because I'm the Doctor. This is what I do.'

Delitsky reached out and caught hold of Bill by the shoulders, pulling her away from the suit. As he did so, the Doctor activated the closing mechanism and there was a whirr of servos as the massive armour closed shut with a clang.

Warning lights started to flash as, under the Doctor's control, the armour came to life and took a few tentative steps across the hangar floor.

'Ooh, tricky.' The Doctor's voice boomed from the speakers, sounding totally inappropriate for the massive mining machine. 'But I think I'll get the hang of it. Right then.' Two armoured gloves rubbed themselves together making the suit seem comically human. 'Shall we go?'

The Ba-El Cratt gestured towards the service lift with its gun. The watching crowd parted as the two machines stamped across the hangar and mounted the short ramp to the lift doors.

As the doors opened, the Ba-El Cratt turned with a final warning for the crew. 'Remember: if an attempt is made to stop our ship from leaving, the Doctor will die.'

The doors slammed shut, and Delitsky gave a massive sigh of relief.

Bill turned to him with a massive grin on her face. 'And the Oscar for best actress in a supporting role goes to Bill Potts!'

Jo Teske clapped Delitsky on the shoulder. 'Well done, Jorgen. I wasn't sure we were going to be able to pull that off.'

Delitsky had to agree. 'I just hope that the Doctor knows what he is doing.'

The Doctor too was breathing a grateful sigh. Grateful that the Cancri had been forced to abandon any kind of visor in the suits, and to rely on external sensors for guidance instead. Whilst it was true that it gave no option for the wearer to see out, it also had the distinct advantage of not allowing anyone on the outside to see in. And that was a very good thing indeed.

He craned his neck, trying to see the subspace tracker that Bill had dropped inside the suit just before he had closed it up. It had come to rest just in front of him, wedged against the buckle of one of the restraining straps that held him firmly in place. To the Doctor's immense relief, Bill had done exactly as instructed. Not that what he had asked was that difficult on a device that only had two buttons. The green button was glowing softly in the dim interior of the armour. Whereas before it had functioned as a tracking device, now it was a transmitter, sending out a signal on a very, very specific subspace frequency, a frequency that he was hoping could only be easily be detected by two people: Rince and whoever he was communicating with on board the pirate ship.

The doors to the service lift slid open. Huge mechanised tractors were moving the last of the diamond-packed cylinders from the vault to the airlock of the Ba-El Cratt ship. Empty, the cavernous space seemed even larger than the Doctor remembered from the last time he had stood here.

His suit was jolted sharply as he was pushed roughly out of the lift and directed towards the airlock. Still coming to terms with the complex controls of the pressure armour, the Doctor made his way gingerly forward, making sure each step was grounded before taking the next.

The two Ba-El Cratt in the vault called out in rough guttural tones to their newly arrived comrade. Their words were unintelligible but their meaning was clear. They wanted to leave.

Urged on by the three aliens, the Doctor made his way inside the airlock. Like the rest of the Ba-El Cratt ship, the cargo lock had a disquieting organic quality, the clean lines of the human-designed diamond cylinder looking uncomfortable next to the swirling, black alien shapes.

As the last of the cargo movers retracted back into the vault, the airlock started to close, petal-like doors almost slithering from the wall before locking together and plunging the room into total darkness.

The Doctor activated his searchlights, then watched as the holographic display hovering in the air in front of his face tracked the pressure build-up outside his suit as the airlock equalised.

Another set of organic doors peeled open ahead of him and, as the Doctor stepped out into the bowels of the alien ship, he was aware of the three other suits of pressure armour springing open like jack-in-the-boxes. With a swirl like an angry tide, the Ba-El Cratt surged past him.

Delitsky watched the monitor screen in subdued awe as the Ba-El Cratt ship swung away from the airlock, looking more like some denizen of the deep ocean than any spacecraft he had ever seen.

'It almost seems alive,' said Bill, echoing his thoughts.

Jo Teske's observation was far more morbid. 'It's horrible. It looks … cancerous, like a tumour.'

Delitsky wished that she could have chosen her words with a little more care. 'It could prove to be just as fatal,' he said grimly, 'if Mr Rince's friends aren't punctual …'

Under the watchful eye of Captain Palmer and Sergeant Harrison, Rince was sitting at the far side of the control room, hunched over the subspace transmitter that had been recovered from his quarters, talking urgently into the microphone.

'Ringbearer to Raptor. The package is moving. I repeat, the package is moving. Target tracer frequency encoded in this transmission. Acknowledge, please.'

As with all the previous attempts he had made, there was still no reply from his unseen collaborators. Rince looked up helplessly.

'Try again,' ordered Delitsky.

'But they're not responding.'

'Try again,' the Rig Chief repeated. 'You got anywhere else to be?'

Rince turned back to the transmitter, repeating the same thing over and over. 'Ringbearer to Raptor. The package is moving. Acknowledge please.'

The Ba-El Cratt ship was starting to accelerate away from them, banking slightly as it started to manoeuvre.

'They're not going to arrive in time, are they?' said Jo, her eyes glued to the screen.

Bill grabbed her hand and squeezed it. 'Trust me. The Doctor can do this.'

Delitsky said nothing. He had no doubts about the Doctor's abilities. Unfortunately, their lives now also relied on the actions of a manager from the Kollo-Zarnista Mining Corporation and his 'friends', and that gave him little comfort.

The Doctor watched with interest as the Ba-El Cratt swirled around him, clearly luxuriating in their freedom after so long confined to their borrowed suits of pressure armour. In their natural form, the aliens were beautiful – fluid and black, their skin rippling with iridescent colour, like a skin of oil on a pool of water.

As they twisted and writhed, it became clear why they had discarded the need for individual names: there were points in this strange dance where it became impossible to separate one creature from the other, the thick viscous gel of their bodies merging and blending, before separating again in a burst of movement. The Ba-El Cratt had obviously developed a complex method of communicating with each other that went well beyond the restrictions of their spoken language.

The frantic dance started to subside, and the creatures began to move around the control room in an intricate pattern, sliding in and out of the holes and fissures in the walls, operating the ship in exactly the manner that the Doctor had supposed. He could feel the tilt of the vessel as it started to bank.

'So, now that you've had a chance to stretch your legs, do you mind telling me where you are taking me?'

One of the Ba-El Cratt oozed from a hole in the floor and drifted towards him. Somehow the Doctor knew that this was the creature that had inhabited Baines's suit.

'Count yourself lucky, Doctor. Your selfless act of bravery has saved your life. For the moment, at least.'

'You intend to destroy the mine,' said the Doctor matter-of-factly.

'Of course we do! It will take a few moments to power up the necessary systems, then we shall target the gravity inverters and the mine will be drawn into the planet's atmosphere and destroyed.' The creature's voice hardened. 'A taste of what will come when we return in force.'

'Yes … Yes, that's what I thought you would do.'

The creature was still for a moment. 'So, your act of bravery was in fact an act of self-preservation? You suspected our intentions and took the child's place simply to save your own life?' The gelatinous form started to quiver in a manner that could only be interpreted as amusement. 'I have been underestimating you, Doctor. Perhaps I will keep you alive just long enough to show the Collective just how duplicitous and unpredictable the people of your planet can be!'

As the Ba-El Cratt curled back towards its fellows the Doctor glanced down at the green light blinking steadily on the front of the tracking device.

'Oh, yes,' he murmured. 'Unpredictable is my middle name.'

Chapter
19

'Ah!' Rince gave a cry of surprise as the subspace transmitter suddenly chirped into life. 'They're responding!'

Bill hurried with the others to the console.

'Let's hear it,' snapped Delitsky.

Sergeant Harrison opened up the monitor channel that she and Robbins had hooked up, and an angry female voice filled the control room.

'Ringbearer, this is Raptor, what the hell are you playing at? The plan was that you give us fair warning, not wait until the package was on its way.'

'It's not my fault,' stammered Rince. 'They moved the schedule forward.'

'And you couldn't give us any more notice than this?' There was a harsh expletive. *'When this is over, we are going to have a long talk about what this means for your percentage.'*

There was a long pause. Delitsky shot a concerned glance across at Palmer. The security captain was obviously thinking the same way. Was the short notice enough of a problem for them to abandon their plans?

'*Why can't we get a sensor lock on the freighter?*'

Delitsky looked pointedly at Rince, reminding the nervous junior executive of what they had agreed he should say.

'They … um …' Rince was starting to sweat. 'They're testing a new sensor dampener.'

There was another expletive. '*Something else that you just forgot to mention?*'

'The homing sensor is in place, though!' gabbled Rince. 'You can still target on that.'

'*You had better be right or, I swear to God, when I see you, I'm going to kill you. Raptor out.*'

Rince collapsed back in his seat, face in his hands.

Delitsky felt a brief pang of sympathy for the man. Even if by some miracle this worked and he avoided being blown up with the rest of them, Rince's choices were a lifetime on a Federation penal colony or a lifetime trying to hide from the pirates that he had just double crossed. Tough call.

'They're coming.' Claire Robbins had been waiting at the sensor console, scanning for any sign of the raiders' ship.

All eyes turned to stare at the main screen.

'Good luck, Doctor,' Delitsky murmured.

The spacecraft was no product of the shipyards of Mars or Ganymede. It had not been designed to be beautiful, or fuel-efficient, or user-friendly. It had been thrown together from the scavenged remains of dozens of other ships with just one purpose: to be fast and deadly.

It swept into the orbit of Saturn at speeds that the engineers at the commercial shipyards would scarcely have believed possible, its engines configured to ignore all the safety parameters that most ordinary people would consider vital to their wellbeing.

But the crew of the spacecraft were not ordinary people. Like the ship itself, they had been thrown together piecemeal, their lives intersecting in dozens of different ways, on trajectories from dozens of different planets, but all leading to this moment.

Guided by the subspace beacon, the raiders' ship bore down on the twisted black shape of the Ba-El Cratt spacecraft. There was no expert pilot at the controls, no Academy graduate with years of Federation flight training behind them. But what did that matter when you could rely on the automatics to do the hard work for you?

The crew inside might have raised an eyebrow at the strange design of the ship they were approaching, but any doubts they might have had vanished with thoughts of the diamonds that lay within. Swooping low over the rings of Saturn, they fired a shot across the bows.

The Ba-El Cratt spacecraft lurched violently as blaster fire glanced off its hull. The Doctor staggered, barely keeping his balance inside the pressure armour as the floor bucked beneath his feet.

To their credit, the Ba-El Cratt reacted instantly, abandoning their planned attack run on the Kollo-Zarnista mine to respond to this new threat. The ship banked alarmingly, and the Doctor was flung against a wall. He hauled himself upright, watching the readings on the pressure suit's HUD as energy discharges coming from the ship spiked again and again. With each spike on the readout the floor shook with a deep, booming vibration. As he'd hoped, the Ba-El Cratt were returning fire.

The Doctor gave a nod of satisfaction, then turned the settings on his gravity inverters to maximum, crossed his fingers, and took a deep breath.

The raiders' spacecraft twisted and span as fire spat from the weapons of the Ba-El Cratt ship, energy tearing through space and smashing into the rings, erupting into vast boiling fireballs as rocks and icebergs were shattered into fragments.

On board, surprise at the severity of the retaliation swiftly turned to blind rage and, as the ship swung about, all thoughts of moderation and mercy vanished and the pirates opened fire with everything that they had.

The Doctor had never been in the centre of an explosion this big before, and it was an experience that he would not be in any hurry to repeat.

As the plasma bolts from the pirates' ship fractured the hull, the Ba-El Cratt spacecraft came apart in silent but spectacular fashion. No longer contained, the huge pressures inside the ship erupted outwards, the explosive decompression literally tearing the ship to pieces in the process. The Ba-El Cratt themselves had barely had time to realise what was happening to them as they boiled away to nothing, gaseous tendrils sucked out into the vacuum of space before dissipating for ever.

In the midst of the fury was the Doctor, his body shaken inside the pressure armour like a bead in a baby's rattle. Over and over he tumbled, pieces of the hull sparking and fizzing around him as the gravity bubble protecting the suit deflected them. All external sensors went dead, life-support systems diverting every scrap of power, concentrating everything towards keeping the occupant of the armour alive.

Slowly, mercifully, the chaos started to subside, and the Doctor was finally able to gain some control, expertly modifying the gravity inverters to finally bring his dizzying spin to a halt.

Head still swimming, the Doctor reactivated his external camera. He hung in space, Saturn a vast swirling ball far beneath his feet, the rings arcing above him, seemingly going on for ever. He was utterly alone. The pirates had obviously fled, either scared away or damaged by the ferocity of the explosion. Of the Ba-El Cratt ship there was nothing, not a single trace save for a faint radiation flare that lingered in his sensor readings. But floating all around him, glinting in the light from the distant Earth, were diamonds.

Millions and millions of diamonds.

Bill sat in the co-pilot's seat of the transport shuttle *Glamorgan*, eyes glued to the window, looking for any trace of the Doctor. They had been searching for nearly an hour now.

Delitsky had initially wanted to wait for a rescue team from Titan to arrive, but Bill had no intention of just sitting and waiting. The shuttle pilot, Tobins, had agreed with her, all too willing to do whatever he could to help the man who had saved all their lives.

Back at the rig, Captain Palmer had Nettleman and Rince locked in the brig and was writing up a detailed report for her superiors. Jo had turned a corner of the gym into a temporary medical bay and was busy treating the injuries – both mental and physical – that had been caused by the Ba-El Cratt. Delitsky was trying to oversee repairs to the station, and deal with a seemingly never-ending series of demands for information from his bosses and from the Federation.

He was also due to give the eulogy at a ceremony that Jenny Flowers was organising to remember Baines and the six crew who had died during the explosion in med-bay. Bill wondered if Jenloz would be included in that speech.

The military cruiser from Ganymede was due to dock in about twenty minutes, and Bill suspected that that was when things would really get busy for Delitsky. She hoped that all turned out well for him. He was a good man.

In the meantime, they had still had no contact with the Doctor. There had been several tense minutes following the explosion of the Ba-El Cratt spacecraft when they had struggled to find him. When the steady pulse from his tracer had finally been located, the entire control room had erupted into cheers.

Now they were just searching through an endless sea of stars for some sign of him. The signal from the subspace transmitter was still beeping away steadily on the console, and the shuttle was still on course, but finding one single tiny figure …

'There he is!'

Bill scrambled out of her seat as Tobin pointed at a glint of light off in the distance. As the shuttle pulled close, the suited figure raised an arm in greeting.

Bill waved back.

Tobin grinned at her. 'I'd better let the mine know.' He reached for the communicator. 'Kollo-Zarnista control, this is the *Glamorgan*.'

'*Reading you*, Glamorgan. *Did you get him?*'

'Yeah, we've got him.'

'*Great news, Tobin.*' Bill could hear the relief in Claire Robbins' voice. '*How's our survivor doing?*'

'OK, as far as we can see. Looks like his comms system is out. I'm going to open the cargo bay doors and get him aboard. I'll let you know when we're on our way back.'

Tobins began to manoeuvre the shuttle so that it was underneath the Doctor. A low vibration rattled Bill's seat as the cargo doors slowly slid open. Using the thrusters on his suit, the Doctor started to make his way to the cargo bay.

Tobins turned to Bill. 'You'd better get back there to help him get out of that suit.'

Bill unhooked her harness and hurried from the cabin, making her way through the short access corridor to the cargo bay door. She waited impatiently as the bay doors closed and the ship re-pressurised the compartment.

With a hiss, the cargo bay door slid open to reveal the Doctor, his armour already starting to unlock and unhinge.

Bill hurried forward. 'Doctor, are you OK?'

'Oh, you know, just been in the middle of an explosion, been left orbiting Saturn for an hour, probably no tea on this shuttlecraft … Typical day, really.'

Bill smiled. The Doctor was doing his best to be his usual testy self, but she could hear the strain of recent events showing in his voice.

'Actually, I've started to realise that this actually *is* a fairly typical kind of day for you.'

'Yes.' He smiled. 'It can be.'

'Doctor …'

248

'Hmm?'

'I think I'm ready to go home now.'

He didn't argue with that, just held out a gloved hand. 'Here.'

Bill reached out for whatever it was the Doctor was holding and he dropped it into her palm.

Bill just stared at the diamond.

'Just do me one favour ...' said the Doctor wearily

She looked at him curiously. 'Of course.'

'When we do get back home, please don't mention any of this to Nardole.'

Bill began to laugh.

Epilogue

Laura Palmer signed off her report and gave a deep sigh. Her first couple of days back on duty had turned out to be quite eventful. The Federation had discovered that it was involved in a war of which it had no knowledge, and the implications were far reaching. A formal complaint had been made to the Cancri about their actions, and there were already rumours that Earth might sever all ties with them rather than risk further conflict with the Ba-El Cratt. Personally, Laura doubted that would happen. The diamonds were too important to the economy. It was far more likely that the military would become involved, strengthening the Federation borders, preparing for another possible Ba-El Cratt incursion. She had already seen draft plans for an intelligence-gathering mission to find the Ba-El Cratt home world. It was going to get messy.

She got up from her chair and stretched, her back aching from being hunched over her terminal for so long. She needed a walk.

Leaving Harrison in charge, she made her way down to the shuttle bay, making her presence known to the technicians on duty, and wandering across the empty landing pad to the observation window on the far side. Strictly speaking, no one was allowed in here when a shuttle arrival was imminent, but she still had plenty of time before Tobins docked the *Glamorgan*, and the guys in traffic control had got used to her strange obsession.

The shuttle bay was one of the few places on board that actually had any kind of window. When the rig was at mining depth, there was very little point in having them – like visors on the suits of pressure armour, they were a potential weak point, and the only view that they offered was of the choking clouds that made up the Saturnian atmosphere.

When the mine was at shallow depths, either for repairs as it was now, or for the loading of offloading of the diamond cargo, then the massive steel shutters that covered those windows were retracted, allowing the crew additional visibility during complicated docking manoeuvres, and affording an unparalleled view of the planet below.

Those shutters were open now, and Laura leaned her forehead on the thick Plexiglas, staring out at the view. Despite the horror of the last twenty-four hours, the sight of Saturn was still enough to send her heart soaring.

She craned her neck, peering up at the rings. Somewhere amongst all that beauty a fortune in gemstones was slowly drifting, a vast cloud of gleaming crystals, inexorably being pulled and shaped by the forces of gravity. In time there would be a new ring around the planet she called home.

A diamond ring.

Acknowledgements

Thanks to Justin Richards and Albert DePetrillo for bringing me on board.

To James Dudley and Edward Russell for arranging a sneak peek at Bill ahead of time.

To Cavan and Jonny, co-conspirators.

To Steffan Morris for opening a door back into the Doctor's world once more.

To Matt Doe for his patience.

To Moogie and Baz.

And to Karen and her hedgehog army, for endless love and support.